dreadnought

Also by Mark Walden

H.I.V.E.: Higher Institute of Villainous Education
H.I.V.E.: The Overlord Protocol
H.I.V.E.: Escape Velocity

H·I·V·E

BLOOMSBURY

LONDON BERLIN NEW YORK

Bloomsbury Publishing, London, Berlin and New York

First published in Great Britain in 2009 by Bloomsbury Publishing Plc
36 Soho Square, London, W1D 3QY

A CIP catalogue record of this book is available from the British Library

ISBN 978 0 7475 9484 0

Typeset by Dorchester Typesetting Group Ltd
Printed in Great Britain by Clays Ltd, St Ives Plc

1 3 5 7 9 10 8 6 4 2

www.bloomsbury.com
www.bloomsbury.com/HIVE
www.markwalden.net

For Mum and Dad.
Thank you.

chapter one

The young girl ran through the knee-deep snow, her breath escaping in ragged gasps, leaving a trail of thin white cloud that hung in the air. She could hear the sounds of pursuit all too close behind her, the barks and snarls of dogs and the coarse shouts of the men who followed them. She could hardly feel her bare feet and lower legs any more as she plunged on through the deep icy powder, the dark ancient trees of the forest surrounding her in all directions. She wore nothing but a tattered dark blue dress made of a rough material that offered little protection from the biting cold.

As she ran over the crest of a small hill, the girl tripped on a rock concealed beneath the blanket of snow and fell, tumbling down the slope. Staggering to her feet, she spotted the vague outline of a cottage, its dark walls half buried beneath deep white drifts. She stumbled towards it, desperately rattling the handle of its only door. It was locked.

The girl gritted her teeth and kicked the wooden door hard, ignoring the pain in her foot. The door refused to budge. She cursed under her breath and kicked again, harder. The ancient lock gave way and as the door flew inwards the girl half staggered, half fell inside. She quickly shut the door behind her and looked around the darkened room. It was obviously a hunting lodge: stuffed animal heads were mounted on the walls and animal skins were scattered on the floor and chairs, but there were no signs of life. Everything was covered by a thick layer of dust which the girl disturbed as she frantically searched the ground floor for anything she could use as a weapon.

Outside, several men in heavy cold-weather outfits ran towards the cottage, led by the vicious snarling dogs straining at the leashes they held.

'The trail ends here,' the first man said in Russian. 'She's inside.'

'Go get her,' said the tall man at the rear of the group. The men on either side of him unslung the rifles that hung across their backs and headed towards the house. They pushed the door open and cautiously entered. Seconds later a single shot rang out from somewhere inside the cottage. Then silence returned to the snow-covered forest.

'Vasilly? Gregor?' the tall man called out, but there was no reply. 'Send the dogs in,' he said with a frown.

Two large, heavily muscled dogs sprinted across the snow and into the cottage. There was sudden noisy barking and then a quick panicked whimpering sound before silence descended once again.

'What should we do, Mr Furan?' one of the dog handlers asked, staring at the darkened windows of the cottage.

'Wait here,' the tall man replied and pulled a handgun from his belt. He walked towards the house and went inside.

'How old is she?' the first dog handler asked.

'I don't know,' the other man replied. 'Ten, eleven years old maybe?'

'She's not going to make it to twelve if Furan has anything to say about it.'

Suddenly, there was a pained yell from inside the house and one of the windows shattered, exploding outwards in a shower of glass as a wooden stool flew through it. The girl dived out through the jagged hole and rolled to her feet, sprinting off through the snow, darting between the trees. Furan staggered out of the cottage, blood streaming from under the hand clutched to his right eye. He raised the pistol and took careful aim at the fleeing girl. He squeezed the trigger, the shot seeming unusually loud in the quiet of the snowy forest.

The girl spun, the bullet striking her in the shoulder, and she collapsed on to the snow. She tried to struggle to her feet but Furan was already on her, pistol-whipping her to the ground, knocking her out cold.

Furan stared down at the unconscious body of the pale, dark-haired girl with his one good eye. The fresh blood stained the snow crimson beneath her shoulder. Her breathing was laboured. He raised the pistol, pointing it at her head. He stood there for a moment, blood dripping from his ruined eye, seemingly unsure whether or not to pull the trigger before he slowly lowered the weapon.

'No, Natalya,' he said, his voice cold and hard, 'that would be too easy. Rest assured though, you won't escape again. This will be your last flight, my little Raven.'

☻ ☻ ☻

twenty years later

State trooper Sam Fletcher was having a bad night. He knew he'd drawn the short straw when he'd been dispatched to the old gas station on the desert road. Mrs Trenton had called to complain, as she did at least three or four times every month, that she was being harassed again by mysterious flying objects and lights in the sky. Sam had known it would be a waste of time, but the Sheriff had insisted that he go and check on the batty old woman. She'd been all alone since her husband had passed away recently and the Sheriff was a friend of the family, which explained why Sam had ended up being sent out there at that time of night. He'd sat in the old woman's front room while she went on about the strange noises she kept hearing and the lights she kept seeing in the sky. On that particular evening she complained that something had flown low right over the house and scared the living daylights out of her as she'd been feeding her chickens in the backyard.

Sam had dutifully listened to her ramble on and had eventually left, promising her that he would look into it and see if the local US Air Force base knew anything about the mysterious aircraft. It would be a futile task; in this part of Nevada they were no strangers to unusual aerial activity, but the kinds of aircraft that were being tested around those parts were not the sort that the air force would be prepared to discuss with someone like Sam. Chances were that some bored fighter jockey had buzzed the Trenton place at a lower altitude than was technically permitted just to liven up a test flight. It wouldn't be the first time something like that had happened and he was fairly sure that it wouldn't be the last. With a weary sigh, he reached for the radio on the dashboard and spoke into the handset.

'Dispatch, this is Car Four, come in, over,' he said.

'Hey, Sam, you rounded up those little green men that have been spooking Clara yet?' the voice at the other end asked.

5

'Yeah, got myself three genuine extra-terrestrials cuffed in the back of my car right now, Maggie,' he replied. 'Matter of fact I – WOAH!'

The trooper jerked the steering wheel hard to the left as his headlights suddenly illuminated a dishevelled figure running straight down the middle of the road towards him. The car's tyres screeched in protest and he dropped the radio handset, both hands flying to the wheel as he fought to control the wildly fishtailing patrol car. Cursing under his breath, he brought the car to a shuddering halt on the side of the road. He stopped for a moment to gather himself and let out a long, deep breath before grabbing his flashlight and stepping out of the car. The powerful beam of the torch lit up the man who Sam had just narrowly avoided running over as he staggered towards the car.

'Sir, please stay right there,' Sam shouted, his other hand resting on the holstered pistol on his hip. 'You know how close I came to hitting you? Care to explain what you're doing running down the middle of the road way out here at this time of night?'

'Please, you have to help me,' the man said. Sam couldn't quite place his accent but it sounded European. 'They're out there, they're after me, they could be here any minute.'

Sam's first instinct had been that he was dealing with

some drunken bum who'd somehow got stranded in the middle of nowhere, but there was something strange about this man. His face was covered in desert dust but he was clean shaven and his hair was neatly trimmed. His clothes were also covered in dirt but the suit he was wearing was well cut and his shoes were expensive. In fact the more that Sam looked at him the less he seemed like someone that you'd expect to find wandering around in the desert twenty miles from the nearest town.

'Who's after you?' Sam asked, walking slowly towards the man.

'The Disciples,' the man said, his eyes filled with fear. 'I know what they're planning. We have to stop them – the government must be warned.'

Not a drunk, but a religious nut, Sam thought to himself.

'What's your name, sir?' Sam asked.

'Tobias Scheckter,' the man replied, looking nervously up at the sky.

'OK, Mr Scheckter, can you tell me what exactly you're doing out here on your own at this time of night?'

'I'm a geologist,' Scheckter replied. 'I have been working for some men, doing calculations, just theoretical. Or at least I thought so . . . oh God. I have to get to a phone,' he continued frantically, 'or a radio. Let me use your radio.'

'Just calm down, sir,' Sam replied. 'Let's take you back to town and see if we can't sort this all out.'

'You don't understand. There's no time!' the man yelled, lunging towards him.

Sam stepped to one side and used the man's own momentum against him, just as he'd been trained to do, forcing the struggling figure to the ground and reaching for the cuffs clipped to the back of his belt.

'I'm afraid you just earned yourself a night in one of our holding cells,' he said, snapping the cuffs closed on the man's wrists. He dragged the stranger to his feet and quickly bundled him into the back of the car, then climbed into the driver's seat. The man in the back was muttering to himself in a foreign language that Sam didn't recognise. He started the car and set off down the road towards town with a sigh: this night was just getting better all the time.

☻ ☻ ☻

'Do we have him?' the voice asked over the loudspeaker mounted in the centre of the control console.

'Yes, we have a biometric match but he appears to have made contact with a local police officer,' the thin man seated at the console replied. He pushed at the joystick he held in one hand and the grainy image of the police cruiser on the road below sharpened as the camera zoomed in. 'What are your orders?'

'Terminate him immediately,' the voice replied. 'He knows too much.'

'Very well,' the thin man replied. He pressed a button on the console and the car was highlighted by a green box. Then he lifted the transparent plastic guard that covered a large red switch labelled with the single word 'COMMIT' next to the joystick .

'Do svidaniya, comrade,' the man at the console said with a small, sadistic smile.

High above the Nevada desert the sleek black unmanned drone banked towards its target. The heat from the car's engine far below gave the on-board computers a perfect infrared target against the cold expanse of the desert surrounding it. The spherical unit mounted under the drone's nose rotated and painted the target with an invisible beam of laser light, as a hatch slid open in the aircraft's belly and a missile dropped down and locked into place. Moments later the missile detached from the drone and fell away, its rocket motor igniting only when it was several metres below the launch platform. The inertial guidance system steered it flawlessly along the invisible laser beam that the drone was projecting and mere seconds later it speared into the roof of the police car, the eight kilogram shaped charge in its nose detonating and consuming the vehicle in a ball of fire. Blazing fragments scattered across the road, pieces tumbling across the cold desert floor and igniting the coarse scrub that dotted the barren landscape.

As silence returned to the desert, a burning debris field was the only sign of the two men's futures that had just been snuffed out and the secret that had cost them both their lives.

☢ ☢ ☢

'Who is she?' Otto asked quietly, looking down at the girl sat alone on one of the sofas in the atrium of their accommodation block.

'I am not sure,' Wing replied. 'All I have heard is that she is joining the Alpha stream.'

Otto already knew that much, but, as far as he was able to determine, that in itself was extremely unusual. New Alphas were inducted annually into the first year; they were never admitted into a more senior year. Not before now, at least. Clearly there was something about this girl that was special and Otto was determined to find out what.

'Perhaps the girls will know more,' Wing said with a nod towards Laura and Shelby, who were approaching from the other end of the corridor.

'Stalking the new girl, Malpense,' Shelby said, jabbing him in the ribs with her finger. 'You do know how creepy that is, don't you?'

'It's not stalking,' Otto replied, 'it's surveillance.'

'Just getting creepier,' Shelby said with a mock shudder.

'Has anyone actually gone and spoken to the poor girl yet?' Laura said, sounding slightly cross. 'I don't suppose anyone's stopped to think about what it was like for us on our first day here. At least then we were all newbies together. Just try and imagine what this must be like for her all on her own. Shelby and I are going to go and say hello. You coming?'

'OK, OK,' Otto said, holding up his hands. 'Let's go and roll out the H.I.V.E. welcome wagon.'

'There's a wagon of some kind?' Wing asked, looking confused.

'Come on, big guy,' Shelby said with a grin and pushed Wing ahead of her down the corridor towards the stairs.

'We could always see what information the central server has on her,' Otto said, still looking down at the girl. 'That's if you fancied having a poke around.'

'I hardly think you need my help with that,' Laura said, pulling Otto away from the balcony.

'Nah, I'm trying to lay off the out-of-body experiences at the moment,' Otto said, sounding distracted.

In recent months Otto had discovered that he had a unique ability to interface remotely with electronic devices or data networks. In theory it made him the most efficient hacker on the planet, but the reality was more worrying. More than once he had almost lost himself within the electronic world, which had left him feeling slightly unsure about the actual benefits of his skill. Number One and Sebastian Trent had both sought to reverse the connection in order to control Otto – and both had very nearly succeeded. Now he found himself increasingly wary of allowing anyone else the chance to exert a similar influence over him.

'Besides, you're a natural,' Otto said. Laura had been inducted into H.I.V.E. after hacking into the U.S. goverment's early warning system so that she could use its resources to listen in on the mobile phone conversations of girls who had been picking on her at her previous school.

'It may not be that easy actually,' Laura said with a frown. 'Professor Pike has beefed up a lot of the network security since H.I.V.E.mind . . . well, you know.'

H.I.V.E.mind, the artificial intelligence that had been in charge of H.I.V.E.'s computer systems, had sacrificed himself to help defeat Overlord and to save Otto's life. It was still something that Otto did not really want to think about.

'You mean it might actually be easier to just talk to her then?' Otto said with a grin.

'Shocking, I know,' Laura replied, 'but sometimes the old ways are the best.'

They headed quickly down the stairs and caught up with Wing and Shelby as they crossed the atrium towards where the girl was sitting. She looked up from her binder as the four of them approached. Her long, straight, jet black hair contrasted sharply with her pale skin and deep blue eyes. There was no doubt that she was pretty but there was something else that Otto felt when he saw her, a certain familiarity.

'Hi, I'm Shelby and this big hunk is Wing,' Shelby said with a grin, 'and these are our two resident brainiacs, Laura and Otto. We thought you might need someone to show you around. My guess is if you're feeling anything like I did on the day we arrived then you've got about a million questions and not many answers. Right?'

'It is a little . . . overwhelming,' the girl replied with a shy smile. 'My name's Lucy – Lucy Dexter.'

'It is an honour to make your acquaintance, Miss Dexter,' Wing said, giving a short bow.

'I think he means hi,' Otto said with a grin and nudged Wing.

'Indeed, hi,' Wing said, raising an eyebrow.

'So what do you think of the old place?' Laura asked, gesturing vaguely at the walls surrounding them.

'It's . . . well, I suppose the word is . . . unbelievable,' Lucy replied. She sounded slightly shell-shocked.

'A secret school for the super-villains of the future,

hidden inside a volcano on a remote tropical island –
what's so hard to believe about that?' Otto grinned.

'Aye, sounds perfectly normal to me, which is, you
know, deeply troubling whichever way you look at it,'
Laura added.

Lucy laughed and gestured towards the folder she'd
been flicking through.

'I've been given the tour and I'm working my way
through the induction manual that they gave me but, to
be honest with you, I'm not even really sure why I'm here.
One minute I was at home reading in bed and the next
thing I knew I was waking up on board a helicopter with
some crazy Russian woman.'

'Oh don't worry, we're familiar with the crazy Russian
woman,' Otto laughed. 'One piece of advice though: I
wouldn't call her that to her face.'

'Not if you're a fan of the whole not eating through a
straw thing anyway,' Shelby said, grinning.

'I do not believe that Raven would ever assault a
student without good reason,' Wing said with a frown.

'I know. I was just, you know, exaggerating, because . . .
funny . . . never mind,' Shelby said with a sigh. Otto tried
very hard not to laugh.

'Is it true that you don't get to leave here until you've
finished all six years?' Lucy asked. 'Have you guys really
not been off the island since you arrived?'

'Well, technically that's true,' Laura said, sitting down on the sofa opposite, 'but we've had a couple of . . . erm . . . unofficial excursions in that time, and there's the occasional training mission that's taken us off the island. In fact there's one in a couple of days, so you won't have to wait too long before you see the outside world again. Admittedly it's an Arctic survival course, so the outside world will mainly consist of endless fields of snow and ice, but, still, it's a change of scene at least. Anyway, we always seem to end up back here, one way or another. Why, you're not thinking about leaving us already, are you?'

'No,' Lucy replied quickly, looking slightly nervous, 'it's not that. It's just that . . . well . . . doesn't this place sometimes feel a bit like a prison?' She looked at each of them in turn.

'I suppose it did once,' Otto replied, 'but after a while it started to feel like home. Some of us don't really have very much to go back to in the outside world. Besides which, this lot would be completely lost without me.' Otto grinned.

'Oh aye,' Laura said, rolling her eyes. 'I for one don't know what I'd do without you putting all our lives in danger at least once every few months.'

'Nothing worse than a nice quiet life with no one shooting at you,' Shelby said, flopping down on the sofa next to Laura. 'What would we do without bullet-magnet Malpense?'

'Hey, that's not fair,' Otto said, sounding hurt. 'Sometimes it's knives, or even bombs.'

'Sounds like you lot have had an interesting couple of years,' Lucy said, looking worried.

'Welcome to H.I.V.E.,' Wing replied with only the hint of a smile.

chapter two

Dr Nero sat down at the conference table in his appointed seat and waited patiently as the dome in the centre of the table lit up with a soft white light. Suddenly, other figures materialised out of thin air, seated in the other chairs around the table, some already engaged in conversation. These new holographic telepresence meetings were one of the first innovations that Diabolus Darkdoom had introduced when he had taken command of G.L.O.V.E., the Global League of Villainous Enterprises. It made a certain amount of sense, Nero supposed, avoiding as it did all of the risks associated with assembling the ruling council in one location, but he still couldn't help but feel that there was something missing. There had been a definite value to sitting in the same room as his fellow G.L.O.V.E. commanders, risky as it may have been. It was, after all, much harder to tell when a holographic projection was lying than when you were sat opposite that person in the same room and could see the beads of sweat forming on their forehead.

'Good morning, ladies and gentlemen.' The figure of Diabolus Darkdoom, the commander of G.L.O.V.E., materialised at the head of the table, immediately to Nero's left. 'I'm glad you were all able to attend this meeting at such short notice. A matter has arisen that requires urgent discussion. You will have noticed, no doubt, that there is an empty seat at the table today, and it is the fact that this seat is unoccupied that has forced me to call us all together.

'Jason Drake has chosen to boycott this meeting for reasons that are not yet entirely clear. I'm well aware that he has expressed discontent with my leadership but it would seem that he has now decided that he no longer wishes to be part of our organisation. G.L.O.V.E. has never tolerated the existence of factions or splinter groups that may compete with our goals and I do not intend to make an exception here. What I need to know now is whether any of you are aware of Drake's intentions. If he is working to establish his own organisation, then I must know now so that we can take appropriate measures.'

Diabolus looked around the table at each of the remaining council members, but no one appeared to be willing or able to give any further information. Nero found himself once again cursing the fact that the low resolution of the holographic projections around the table made it difficult, if not impossible, to see the tiny clues of expression or body language that might have revealed which of them knew more than they were prepared to say.

'Very well,' Diabolus said firmly. 'If Drake is indeed planning to set up a new organisation, it may be that he will approach some of you for support. I'm sure I do not need to explain to any of you what the consequence would be if I were to find out that you were secretly conspiring with him.'

'What makes you so sure he's gone rogue?' Carlos Chavez, chief of G.L.O.V.E.'s South American operations, asked.

'I have, or should I say had, sources close to Drake,' Darkdoom replied. 'Those sources have fallen silent, but not before they informed me that some form of operation was being planned and that this organisation was the target.'

'Do we know where he intends to strike?' Madame Mortis asked.

'No, we do not,' Darkdoom replied. 'So I suggest all of you increase your levels of security. Any activities that you have scheduled could be jeopardised, so you may want to delay or cancel them. I leave it to your discretion.'

'He's a public figure, the head of a multinational corporation,' Baron Von Sturm said. 'He can't disappear for ever.'

'Oh, I have no doubt he will resurface,' Darkdoom said, 'and when he does, Doctor Nero will be asking Raven to have a little chat with him, won't you, Max?'

'Of course.' Nero nodded. He was pleased to see the slightly nervous expressions on the other faces at the table. Raven was his most trusted operative and also the world's most feared assassin. Nobody at this meeting ever wanted to find themselves at the top of her to-do list.

'Now, I'm certain that we all have other things we need to attend to, so I won't keep you any longer. Needless to say, if any of you hears anything, I expect you to inform me immediately. Understood?'

The other heads of global villainy gathered around the table nodded.

'Very good,' Darkdoom said. 'Do Unto Others.'

'Do Unto Others,' the members of the council said, repeating G.L.O.V.E.'s motto, and one by one the projected images of the council members around the table flickered and vanished, until only Nero and Darkdoom remained.

'You have something to add, Max?' Darkdoom said, looking irritated.

'You realise how dangerous this could be, I assume?' Nero asked calmly.

'Of course I do,' Darkdoom snapped before taking a deep breath and slumping back in his chair. 'I'm sorry, this situation has rather caught me by surprise.'

'You knew he was unhappy,' Nero said. 'We all did. There was always going to be those who were unhappy with your appointment as head of the council. Number One may have sought to betray us all, but it didn't mean that everyone disagreed with the way he ran G.L.O.V.E. Drake wanted the seat that you're sitting in for himself and he was never going to be content to just take orders from you. We all knew that.'

'Maybe, but he was one of the most powerful members of the ruling council in terms of manpower and resources. To lose him now, when we're still vulnerable . . .'

Nero understood what Darkdoom meant. It was not easy to satisfy the technological requirements of an organisation like G.L.O.V.E. without having existing legitimate production facilities that could be discreetly used to manufacture the equipment they needed. Jason Drake was the head of Drake Industries and had been responsible for developing much of the advanced technology that G.L.O.V.E. used on a daily basis. To lose access to the resources he had at his disposal had the potential to be catastrophic in itself, quite aside from any other plans Drake might have to cause harm to the organisation.

'G.L.O.V.E. will endure, it always has,' Nero said reassuringly. 'We just have to make sure this situation doesn't devolve into civil war. If I know Drake, his first course of action will be to try to recruit the remaining members of the council, or turn them against one another – assuming, of course, that he hasn't already.'

'You think that we may have traitors in our midst?' Darkdoom asked, gesturing at the empty seats around the table.

'No member of this council got where they are today by using honour and fair play, including us, so we shouldn't be surprised if they are trying to work out how they might best profit from this situation. We just need to make sure we stay one step ahead of the game.'

Darkdoom nodded thoughtfully.

'Thank you, Max. I can always rely on you to watch my back, at least.'

'Trust is everything now,' Nero replied, looking Darkdoom straight in the eye. 'This is going to get worse before it gets better. That much at least we can be certain of. Drake wouldn't have taken a step like this unless he had some reason to feel secure from G.L.O.V.E.'s wrath. Von Sturm was right: he's too public a figure to just disappear. He knows he'll have to come back up for air, but I fear that means that whatever he has planned is designed to remove us as a threat to him before he does.'

Darkdoom let out a long sigh and rubbed at his temples with both hands.

'You know, in all my years in hiding I had forgotten

what sitting at this table was like,' he said, sounding tired. 'Number One made it look easy.'

'Number One was a psychopathic artificial intelligence,' Nero said. 'I don't think there was very much to admire about him.'

'Not always, Max,' Darkdoom said. 'He started out as human as you or me. We should not forget what he achieved before Overlord corrupted him. He founded this organisation and he kept it from imploding against all the odds for many years. I don't think I'd really appreciated how difficult that must have been until now. Sometimes I wonder if it wouldn't just have been easier to stay dead . . .'

'Be careful what you wish for . . .' Nero said with a crooked smile.

Darkdoom laughed and leant his head back against the headrest of his seat.

'Actually, there was something else I wanted to discuss with you, which is vaguely connected to Drake. The Dreadnought has finished its shakedown mission and is ready for full deployment. I wondered if you'd like to come and take a tour.'

'You and your toys,' Nero said with mock exasperation. The fact of the matter was that the construction of the Dreadnought had been one of the final projects that Drake Industries had completed for G.L.O.V.E.

23

'The Dreadnought isn't a toy; it's one of the most sophisticated vehicles ever built and a vital part of the future of this organisation.'

'Of course it is,' Nero said with a sigh, 'besides which, I think we should meet face to face to discuss these recent developments in greater detail.'

'Agreed,' Darkdoom said, nodding.

'Send me the Dreadnought's coordinates and I'll arrange transport.'

'Excellent. I'll see you soon.'

☻ ☻ ☻

'So one can see that quantum entanglement is a serious issue when it comes to devising effective teleportation techniques, but those very same problems could be usefully harnessed, in theory at least, in the development of effective disintegration technology. I'll go into greater detail about this next week and by then I will expect you to have studied the first three chapters of Igor Kreuzmann's seminal work on offensive beam weaponry, *No, I Expect You To Die*. Class dismissed.'

Professor Pike stepped down from the lectern at the front of the classroom and began to pack his papers into his battered old attaché case.

'Thank God that's over,' Shelby sighed.

'What are you talking about?' Laura said, sounding

genuinely surprised. 'That was fascinating. If we could just figure out the quantile molecular reassembly algorithm . . . well, the sky's the limit.'

'I don't know,' Otto replied, sounding similarly enthused. 'The Einsteinian constraints are so specific in such cases that . . .'

'And so it begins,' Wing said to Shelby and Lucy.

'They'll just rattle on at each other like that for another half hour now,' Shelby groaned as Otto and Laura continued to chatter away. 'They should just figure out a way to directly connect their brains to each other. At least that way none of the rest of us would have to listen to them.'

'I would be careful suggesting such a thing,' Wing said. 'They might just do it.'

'So how did you find your first day?' Shelby asked Lucy as the students began to slowly file out of the classroom and into the corridor.

'I feel like I'm a bit out of my depth, to be honest,' Lucy replied with a small sigh. 'It's a lot to take in at once. I just feel like I've got so much catching up to do.'

'Don't worry,' Shelby said, smiling, 'that feeling only lasts –'

'A couple of years and counting,' Wing interrupted.

'Just ignore tall, dark and grumpy here,' Shelby said, putting her arm around Lucy's shoulders. 'The fact of the matter is that within a couple of weeks all of this will seem quite normal. That's when you know you've really got a problem. But I've found a solution, something that can make all of the weirdness worth putting up with, something I like to call . . . senior boys' water polo practice. Every Wednesday night – bring refreshments.'

'Sounds good,' Lucy said with a smile.

'Oh it is,' Shelby replied. 'I like to think of it as a kind of art form, just with, you know, more rippling wet torsos.'

'Now you're making me feel dirty for attending,' Laura said, having finished her brief quantum dynamics discussion with Otto. 'All I really care about is that H.I.V.E.'s way more interesting than a normal school,' Laura said, 'if a little weirder.'

'I think the Stealth and Evasion lesson was the strangest,' Lucy said. 'Not so much the lesson as the teacher actually. I mean . . . Ms Leon. She's . . . well . . .'

'A cat?' Otto offered with a cheery smile.

'Yeah . . . yeah, that's really the only way of putting it,' Lucy said, sounding slightly bewildered.

'Don't worry, you get used to it,' Shelby said. 'Besides, it's only when the giant mutated flesh-eating plants and android ninjas are around that things really get weird.'

Lucy started to laugh but stopped when she saw the expression on the other students' faces.

'That was a joke, right?' Lucy asked.

'Anyway,' Otto said, breaking into the awkward silence, 'me and Wing have got to go. We've got that thing . . . you know in the library.'

'Oh, yes!' Wing said quickly. 'The thing . . . yes. We must go and do that thing now.'

'Catch you guys later,' Otto said as he and Wing headed off down another corridor.

'What thing?' Laura asked Shelby as the two boys hurried away.

'I dunno,' Shelby said with a knowing smile, 'but it would be a really unfair invasion of their privacy to follow them.'

'Just what I was thinking,' Laura said and the two of them set off after the boys. After a couple of paces they both stopped and turned around.

'You coming?' Shelby asked Lucy, who was standing in the middle of the corridor, looking a bit confused. Lucy gave a small nod and hurried after them.

☣ ☣ ☣

'I am not liking the sound of this,' Franz said, looking over Nigel's shoulder at the monitor on the desk. He flopped down on his bed in their shared room with an explosive sigh.

'Yeah,' Nigel said, pushing his glasses back up on to the bridge of his nose. 'I'm trying to work out what's worse, the Arctic survival course or the fact that our group's going to be supervised by Raven.'

They had known that the course was coming for weeks and while some of the Alphas, like Wing and Shelby, actually seemed to be looking forward to it, most of the stream were viewing it with a mixture of apprehension and fear. Those feelings were not helped by the fact that the older Alpha students referred to this particular part of H.I.V.E.'s curriculum as 'the ninety-three percenter' because that was the proportion of students who returned alive.

'I am being extremely sensitive to cold,' Franz said. 'I have already tried to explain this to Colonel Francisco but he did not seem to care.'

Nigel recalled that particular conversation. It had ended with Colonel Francisco, their Tactical instructor, telling Franz that he had to go on the course just in case something went wrong and the food ran out. The Colonel had then gone on to explain to the rest of the class that they could, in theory, 'live off Franz for a week'. Nigel was *fairly* sure it had been a joke.

'Well, there's no getting out of it now,' Nigel said with a sigh. 'On the positive side, it does mean that we get to leave the island for a few days.' It had been a long time since either of them had left H.I.V.E. and while all their needs were catered for by the school and they lived in relative comfort, it would still be nice to have a change of scenery. Suddenly, the entry buzzer sounded and Nigel got up and pressed the switch to open the door.

'Oh no, not again,' Nigel said as the door hissed open.

Standing outside were Block and Tackle, who, despite stiff competition, were the most notoriously thuggish members of H.I.V.E.'s Henchman stream. H.I.V.E. was sorted into four separate groups, or streams, each containing students who had a unique set of abilities. There was the Political and Financial stream who wore grey uniforms, the Science and Technology stream who wore white uniforms, the Alpha stream, the future leaders of villainous organisations, who wore black uniforms, and finally the Henchman stream. Their blue uniforms were indicators that the only real talent they appeared to have was the ability to break any given bone in your body in the minimum amount of time possible.

'What do you want?' Nigel said irritably.

'We just wondered if there was anything you needed doing?' Block said politely.

'Anything at all,' Tackle added.

Nigel sighed. Up until fairly recently these two would have liked nothing more than to bully or torment Nigel and Franz in some new and inventively sadistic way, but ever since Nigel's father, Diabolus Darkdoom, had become the head of the G.L.O.V.E. ruling council, they had rather substantially changed their tune. Nigel did not exactly miss getting his head flushed down the toilet, but their behaviour was now, in its own way, just as unpleasant.

'No, thanks, I'm fine,' Nigel said with a sigh.

'The bathroom is needing a clean,' Franz piped up from behind Nigel, jerking his thumb at the door at the back of the room.

Block and Tackle looked at each other, clearly unsure what to do.

'No, it's OK, Franz is just joking,' Nigel said, shooting an angry look at his room-mate.

'I am?' Franz replied, slightly surprised.

'Yes, there's nothing we need at the moment but thanks for asking.' Nigel hit the button beside the door and it began to slide closed.

'If there's anything else . . .' Block said.

'Anything at all . . .' Tackle added as the door shut with a clunk.

'I thought I asked you not to do that,' Nigel said to Franz, sitting back down at the desk.

'Do what?' Franz asked innocently.

'You know what I mean,' Nigel snapped. 'After the lunch queue incident you promised me you wouldn't take advantage of my dad's position again.'

'That was just being a minor misunderstanding,' Franz replied quickly.

'You told one of the first years that if they didn't let you cut into the queue, then my father would have Raven assassinate them,' Nigel said angrily.

'Well, he might have done . . .' Franz replied weakly.

'You know, sometimes I really wish people didn't know,' Nigel said, rubbing his temples.

'I'm sorry,' Franz said quietly. 'You are right. I will not do it again. You are knowing that I am not being your friend just because of who your father is, right?'

'Of course I know that,' Nigel said, looking at Franz. 'I just wish I could say the same of everyone else.'

☢ ☢ ☢

'Ow, ow, ow, ow, ow,' Otto yelped, hopping around on his one good foot.

'You allowed your guard to drop. Your enemies will exploit such weaknesses,' Wing said, backing away from Otto and twirling the wooden stave he was wielding back into the ready position tucked under one arm.

'Tell me again why I let you talk me into this?' Otto asked, treading gingerly on his sore foot. Nothing seemed to be broken at least. They may have both been wearing full sparring pads but that didn't mean it didn't hurt.

'Because we have already encountered many situations where the ability to defend oneself has been crucial, and by your own admission your skills in those areas were . . . lacking.'

It was a weakness that Otto knew he had to spend time addressing, but unlike most of his other unique abilities, theory was no use to him now. He had spent hours before this session absorbing all of the information that H.I.V.E.'s library had to offer on self-defence, but a complete working knowledge of nearly every documented fighting style didn't mean that his body knew how to do it. He could learn to pilot a fighter jet in minutes, but it didn't mean he could perform a roundhouse kick, as Wing was capably demonstrating.

'Let's go again,' Wing said.

'Why not? I think there might be a couple of square centimetres of my body that aren't bruised yet,' Otto groaned.

'I'm sorry,' Wing replied. 'Your lips were moving but all I heard was a whining noise.'

'You're really enjoying this, aren't you?' Otto said, adopting the same ready stance as Wing.

'I take no pleasure in it whatsoever,' Wing said with a grin.

Wing advanced again and Otto tried to remember what he had already learnt: keep your balance, understand your centre of gravity and allow instinct to control action but never lose control. Easy to learn, hard to master. He dropped low and swung the staff up at Wing's ribs. Wing's staff snapped across his body, blocking Otto's blow before thrusting the other end between Otto's knees and spinning past him, knocking Otto's feet out from under him and sending him crashing down on to his back. All the breath in Otto's body seemed to leave in one explosive exhalation.

Wing offered Otto his hand and pulled his winded friend back up.

'Are you OK?' Wing asked.

'Can't . . . talk . . . breathing . . .' Otto gasped, trying desperately to suck air back into his lungs.

'What did you forget?' Wing asked.

'To bring a handgun?' Otto replied, pressing gingerly on his ribs.

'I'm not sure even that would have helped, to be honest,' Wing said with a chuckle. 'I think that's enough for today.'

The pair of them headed for the changing rooms and quickly showered and got changed back into their regulation black jumpsuits. They walked out and on to the gallery overlooking the training area, where they found Laura, Shelby and Lucy. The girls broke into spontaneous applause as Otto and Wing approached.

'You were all watching?' Otto asked, wincing.

'You're joking, aren't you?' Laura said. 'I wouldn't have missed this for the world; it's the best show in town. I think it's the combination of comedy and intense violence that makes it such a winner.'

'I made popcorn,' Shelby said, holding up a half-full plastic bowl. 'Want some?'

'You two *are* friends, right?' Lucy asked, gesturing at him and Wing.

'We used to be,' Otto said, 'before we started this *private* training session.'

'Oh come on, Otto,' Laura said with a grin. 'You've got nothing to be ashamed of. Some of that was almost like ballet.'

'Yeah,' Shelby replied, 'just with slightly more blunt-force trauma to the head and neck area than usual.'

'Speaking of trauma,' Laura said, 'everyone ready for our exciting trip to the Arctic Circle tomorrow?'

'It will be an excellent opportunity to test our physical limits,' Wing said happily. 'I am looking forward to it a great deal.'

'And that's despite the fact that I didn't hit him in the head even once,' Otto said quickly. 'Personally I'd rather eat a bucket of broken glass.'

'I'm with Otto,' Laura said with a sigh. 'Give me a warm library and a laptop any day of the week.'

'Hey guys, where's your sense of adventure?' Shelby said with a grin. 'It'll be fun.'

'Woohoo,' Otto said sarcastically. 'Fun – frozen, lonely-death fun.'

'I hope you don't mind,' Lucy said, 'but I asked Colonel Francisco if I could join your group for the training. He said it should be fine but he'd have to check with the person who's supervising your group, someone called Raven.'

'Or "the crazy Russian woman" as she's now known,' Shelby said.

'You know, I'm quite offended that they've put Raven in charge of our group,' Otto said with mock indignation. 'It's almost as if they think we're going to cause trouble.'

'Aye,' Laura said with a smile. 'We don't *cause* trouble. It just, sort of, happens around us.'

☢ ☢ ☢

H.I.V.E.'s crater hangar was bustling with activity as the assembled students were directed to the Shroud dropships assigned to take them to the survival training exercise. Security guards in their distinctive orange jumpsuits patrolled the area, keeping the students under constant close surveillance. Dr Nero made his way across the landing pad and the groups of students quickly fell silent.

'I'm sure you are all eager to be on your way to this training exercise,' Nero said with a slight smile, 'but I wanted to take this opportunity to remind you all of the rules that govern any trip outside of the school. You'll be monitored at all times by your supervising staff member and you'll obey their commands without question. You will be facing one of the most hostile environments on the planet and if you do not follow your instructor's orders then some of you may not survive. Such is the consequence of failure, a lesson that you need to learn well if you're to be future G.L.O.V.E. operatives. Good luck and I hope to see nearly all of you back here in four days' time.' Nero turned to Chief Monroe, the head of H.I.V.E. security. 'You may commence boarding.'

The security guards around the room began to herd the separate groups of Alphas towards the Shrouds, the boarding ramps dropping from beneath the tails of the aircraft as they approached. Otto, Wing, Shelby, Laura, Lucy, Nigel and Franz slowly filed up the ramp and into the passenger compartment. Raven stood at the far end, watching them closely as they took their seats along the bulkheads.

'I can see why they gave me this group,' Raven said, raising an eyebrow.

'And I thought it was because you missed us all so much,' Otto said with a smile.

'That will be quite enough from you, Mr Malpense,' Nero said as he stepped up into the compartment. 'Oh, don't worry,' he continued, seeing their surprised expressions, 'I won't be joining you on the exercise. Enticing a prospect as spending several days in sub-zero temperatures is, I'm just taking advantage of the transportation. I'll be leaving you well before you reach your destination.'

Nero made his way through the compartment, nodding to Raven as he passed, and climbed up the ladder leading to the flight deck above.

'I believe that Doctor Nero was quite clear, but I just want to add something.' She gave them all a smile that would freeze blood. 'Try to escape from *my* supervision and it won't be the hostile environment you have to worry about.' Raven gestured to several crates behind her. 'I need you to perform an in-flight inventory of the equipment here. Once that is done I will give you a more detailed briefing about exactly what the exercise will entail.'

From outside they could hear the distinctive whine of the Shroud's turbines.

'It appears that we are ready to depart,' Raven continued. 'Strap yourselves in for take-off. I will return once we are airborne.'

Raven climbed up the ladder to the flight deck, where she found Nero buckling himself into one of the seats behind the pilot, who was performing his final pre-flight checks.

'Just let me sincerely thank you once again for giving me this group,' Raven said sarcastically as she lowered herself into the seat next to Nero.

'I thought you might appreciate the challenge,' Nero said with a sly smile.

'Interesting to see that they've taken Miss Dexter under their wing,' Raven said as the Shroud began to rise slowly out of the crater.

'Yes,' Nero replied quietly, 'though somehow I doubt they'd be quite so friendly if they knew all the details of her background.'

'Clearly she hasn't discussed it with them yet,' Raven said as she strapped herself into the final spare seat in the cockpit. 'And if she has any sense, she never will.'

chapter three

Jason Drake stood watching as the last of his men filed on to the enormous aircraft that stood on the runway. He was a handsome man in his early forties with short dark hair and an immaculately trimmed goatee beard. He wore an exquisitely cut and obscenely expensive suit that perfectly fitted his position as the CEO of one of the world's most successful technology companies. He had made his first million dollars when he was seventeen years old, selling the first generation of unmanned surveillance aircraft to the air force, and had never looked back. Now Drake Industries was one of the biggest military contractors in the world, specialising in aircraft and satellite technology. Of course the military knew nothing about his 'off-book' projects, like the transport sitting on the tarmac in front of him. It had a passing resemblance to a Shroud dropship, which he had also designed, but it was much larger, with an expanded cargo/passenger compartment and an entire mobile command centre on the upper deck. The dust picked up by the raging desert winds blew in thick clouds across the strip of black tarmac, making it hard to distinguish the outlines of the men as they ascended the ramp into the belly of the aircraft. He glanced at his watch: everything was proceeding precisely on schedule despite the dust storm. A man wearing a desert-camouflage uniform and goggles ran towards him, removing the scarf that had been concealing the lower half of his face.

'Load out should be complete within the next ten minutes, sir,' the man reported, raising his voice over the howling wind. 'The pilot's not too happy about taking off in these conditions though.'

'The pilot will take off as instructed or I will find someone to replace him,' Drake said calmly. 'We have a limited window of opportunity here. There can be no delays.'

'Yes, sir,' the uniformed man replied.

'Has Furan reported in from the facility yet?' Drake asked.

Pietor Furan was a dangerous man, Drake knew that much about him, but he had needed access to a source of reliable mercenaries. They could not be the usual dogs of war; they had to be utterly ruthless and incredibly highly trained for a mission such as the one they were about to undertake. His fellow members of the Disciples had assured him that Furan was the only man for the job. Drake had tried to do a little investigation into Furan's past, but it appeared that no records existed. He knew how difficult and expensive such a lack of records was to arrange and it made him slightly uneasy, but he could not fault the quality of the men that Furan had delivered. The past couple of weeks of training had been intensive and uniquely demanding and they had all risen to the challenge admirably. For the ludicrous amount of money that they were costing him, Drake expected no less.

'Yes, sir, Mr Furan reports that they are ready to receive the delivery,' the man replied.

'Excellent. Nothing can stop us now.' Drake smiled to himself; all his planning of the past months was finally coming to fruition. In just a few short hours a chain of events would be set in motion that would destroy Darkdoom's pathetic new regime and restore the forces of global villainy to the position of terrifying power that it was their right and duty to hold. Some people might have wondered what a man like Drake could possibly have wanted from the world that all his existing power and money could not provide. Their answer would come soon enough.

☻ ☻ ☻

41

The pilot of the Shroud frowned as he looked out through the cockpit window. Huge, angry-looking, black storm clouds filled the sky ahead of them.

'Are you certain that these are the correct coordinates, sir?' the pilot asked, sounding slightly nervous.

'Quite certain,' Nero replied. 'Is there a problem?'

'It's just that if we continue on this course it means flying straight through that.' The pilot pointed at the threatening cloud formation ahead of them just as the first fat drops of rain began to spatter across the window. 'It won't be a smooth ride, by any means.'

'I'll make sure everything is secured below,' Raven said, getting up out of her seat.

'I don't think that will be necessary,' Nero said with a smile and gestured to the approaching storm.

Something remarkable was happening ahead of them. Like a giant pair of curtains, the clouds were parting, creating a clear path through the tempest.

'I don't understand . . .' the pilot said quietly.

As they flew onwards the clouds continued to part until finally they revealed an aircraft quite unlike anything any of them had ever seen before, hovering untouched in the centre of the whirling storm. It looked almost like an advanced type of aerodynamic battleship but with four huge clusters of jet turbines, one mounted at each corner, holding the massive vessel aloft. The superstructure was bristling with weapons and sophisticated sensor equipment and mounted at the front was a huge silver sphere, its surface covered in a sparking white energy field. As the Shroud flew closer, a huge bay door slid open at the rear of the aircraft, revealing a hangar that already contained several other aircraft.

'Incoming Shroud dropship, this is Dreadnought Control, please engage ILS and follow the glide path in,' an unfamiliar voice said over the radio. The pilot quickly complied, banking the Shroud towards the enormous vessel and lining up his approach on the illuminated landing area inside the hangar bay. The Shroud slowly dropped down and landed on the steel deck with a gentle bump as the hangar doors closed behind them.

'What is this thing?' the pilot said as uniformed ground crew approached the Shroud.

'The future of G.L.O.V.E., apparently,' Nero replied, getting up and heading for the ladder to the lower compartment. He couldn't help but smile as he climbed down and saw the puzzled expression on Otto's face.

'Is there something wrong, Mr Malpense?' Nero asked.

'Well, we've just landed,' Otto said with a frown, 'but traditionally aircraft have to descend before they can land.'

'That is quite true,' Nero said with a smile, making his way to the rear of the compartment. There may have been no windows in this part of the Shroud but it was perfectly clear to his students that something strange was going on. Nero hit the switch on the bulkhead and the cargo ramp lowered with a mechanical whine. Waiting at the bottom with a broad smile on his face was Diabolus Darkdoom. He wore an immaculate dark red suit and a black shirt and had the unmistakable aura of power that accompanied all great men and women.

'Good afternoon, Doctor Nero,' Darkdoom said, shaking Nero's hand. 'It's good to see you in the flesh again.' Raven walked down the ramp behind Nero and nodded to Darkdoom. 'Natalya, a pleasure as always.' Darkdoom peered past them into the Shroud. 'And I see you've even brought some of my favourite H.I.V.E. students with you. Hello Nigel, it's nice to see you and your friends again.'

'Hello Father,' Nigel said, looking a bit embarrassed.

'I'm afraid that they cannot stay for long. They're in transit to a training exercise,' Nero said.

'Surely they could be allowed a quick tour of G.L.O.V.E.'s new base of operations,' Darkdoom said. 'After all, they are the future of our organisation and they should see for themselves what we're capable of.'

Nero knew that it was pointless to argue. Like many of the great villains throughout history, Darkdoom could not resist the temptation to show others the extent of his power. It was a weakness that Nero had always resisted; too many of his peers had seen their plans derailed by this tendency to brag. 'I suppose a short tour can do no harm,' he said with a sigh.

'Excellent.' Darkdoom smiled and he walked away from the Shroud, gesturing for them all to follow him.

'Welcome to the Dreadnought, ladies and gentlemen, the world's first permanently airborne defence platform. We are currently cruising at an altitude of thirty thousand feet,' Darkdoom informed the group as they made their way across the hangar, where several other Shroud dropships were parked, ready for deployment. 'The Dreadnought is designed to stay airborne indefinitely and provide G.L.O.V.E. with a permanent command post that is both safe and discreet. She is equipped with thermoptic camouflage systems just like the Shroud dropships but she also has other less *conventional* methods to disguise our location.'

Darkdoom led them out of the hangar and down a corridor that was lined on one side with large windows of thick toughened glass. Outside they could see the distant inner wall of the storm that surrounded the Dreadnought.

'As you can see we have perfected a technology that allows us to harness local weather systems, which in turn enables us to entirely conceal our presence from the eyes of the world. At the other end of the hull is a device

45

known as the Zeus Sphere: it allows us to directly manipulate the climate immediately surrounding the Dreadnought and cloak us in a storm that is fully under our control. Needless to say, this is just the first generation of this technology; in future we will be able to exert ever greater control over the climate. Entire continents will be at our mercy; the power afforded to those who govern both the drought and the flood will be immeasurable. But that is for tomorrow. For today we have a natural barrier that acts as a near impenetrable deterrent to airborne attack.'

Darkdoom continued to lead them through a maze of cramped corridors, occasionally pointing out some technological feature or area of interest while the H.I.V.E. students asked numerous questions. Otto could not help but be impressed as he was shown around the massive ship; it was a staggering feat of engineering. Eventually they arrived on the bridge. There was a central command seat surrounded by consoles where uniformed technicians sat controlling the vital systems of the massive airborne battleship and monitoring the nearby airspace. All around the outside of the bridge were large panoramic windows that offered stunning views of the dark vortex of clouds surrounding them.

'Too long has G.L.O.V.E. been forced to scurry from one hidden bolt-hole to another. The Dreadnought will be a permanent base of operations, somewhere that can give us an unparalleled strategic advantage anywhere in the world.' Darkdoom smiled at the faces of the H.I.V.E. students; it was clear from their expressions that they were impressed by this new weapon in G.L.O.V.E.'s arsenal. 'Any more questions?'

'The power requirements to keep this thing in the air must be enormous,' Otto said, looking at the consoles and displays that surrounded them. 'How are you keeping the lights on?'

'As ever, Mr Malpense, straight to the heart of the matter,' Darkdoom said with a smile. 'The Dreadnought is powered by the world's first functioning fusion reactor. Something of a technological marvel in itself. In essence, we have harnessed the power of a star and as such there is never any need to refuel.'

'Isn't that dangerous?' Laura asked. 'Surely if the core were to overload . . .'

'We have taken every precaution, Miss Brand. This technology, while new, is quite reliable, I assure you,' Darkdoom replied. He glanced at Nero, who discreetly tapped the face of his wristwatch. 'I'm sure you have many other questions, but I fear Doctor Nero is eager for you to continue your journey and he and I have much to discuss. Perhaps you might serve aboard this ship yourselves in a few years' time when you have completed your studies at

H.I.V.E., but for now, I'm afraid, I must return you to Raven's capable hands and wish you a safe journey onwards.'

Nero watched as Raven and the students filed off the bridge, heading back to the hangar bay.

'They are an impressive group, Max. They do you and your school great credit,' Darkdoom said as he watched them leave.

'They are some of our more . . . capable students, certainly,' Nero replied, secretly glad that their tour of the Dreadnought had been completed without incident.

'I'm glad to see that Nigel is well too,' Darkdoom said, 'and that he has friends.'

'Indeed,' Nero said with a wry smile.

'So what do you think of the Dreadnought then?' Darkdoom gestured at the walls around them.

'Most impressive,' Nero replied, 'though it does highlight the fact that it will be almost impossible to build something like this in the future without Drake Industries providing the resources.'

'You worry too much, Max,' Darkdoom said. 'There are plenty of other arms manufacturers in the world and I don't expect it will be too hard to find one whose interests are served by becoming part of our organisation.'

'I suppose so,' Nero replied quietly. 'But imagine if this thing or something like it was placed in the hands of our enemies. Drake is too dangerous to just let him act as a free agent. We have to take action. An example has to be made.'

'I'm well aware of that,' Darkdoom said, 'and on that note I wondered if you might let me borrow Raven for a couple of days when she is finished with this exercise. Rumours are reaching me of Drake's location and I think it would be a good idea if she were to pay him a visit as we discussed.'

'Of course, she is yours to command,' Nero replied quietly. It appeared that Jason Drake was going to find out the hard way just what it cost to betray G.L.O.V.E.

☢ ☢ ☢

High above the artificial storm cell, a giant hatch opened in the tail of the cloaked aircraft that had been shadowing the Dreadnought for nearly an hour. Jason Drake watched as the men that Furan had recruited for him filed towards the opening, each wearing a full bodysuit, helmet and a large, solid-looking black backpack.

'Any sign that they've seen us?' Drake asked one of the men sitting inside the cramped control room at the front of the plane.

'No, sir,' the man responded. 'Radar is still in passive acquisition mode and weapons systems are in standby configuration. If they have seen us they're doing an excellent job of pretending they haven't. Looks like our cloaking systems are functioning perfectly.'

'Give the assault team the go,' Drake ordered and turned back to the view screen. He hit a switch and the view changed to a schematic diagram of the Dreadnought, with several points on the external superstructure clearly highlighted. It had not been difficult to work out the best method for attacking the huge vessel; after all, he had had a hand in designing many of its critical systems.

Drake knew that this was the point of no return. He was taking the final irrevocable step across the line that would mean an outright declaration of war. That was why he intended to strike at Darkdoom directly. The only way to slay such a vicious beast was to lop off its head and Drake was a firm believer in decisive action.

He couldn't help but wonder how things might have turned out differently. When he had first conceived the Dreadnought it had been his dream to present it to Number One as a gift that would secure him a place at his former master's right hand. But then Nero and Darkdoom had struck against Number One and carried out their treacherous coup. He had listened patiently as they had spun their ridiculous story about the Overlord AI secretly being in control of Number One and had recognised it immediately as the cover story for the blatant power grab that it was. Drake had watched in silent fury as Darkdoom had taken over the organisation almost completely unopposed by the ruling council. They could not see how unsuitable he was, how he lacked the ruthlessness and cunning that had made Number One their leader for so long and with such success.

It had been even more galling then when Darkdoom had learnt of the Dreadnought project and declared that he would take control of the vessel and use it as his own personal flagship. Drake had no choice but to allow Darkdoom to take the ship; he had not been in a position at that point to openly defy him and the council, but that was all about to change. He had new backers now. A new organisation that was even more powerful than G.L.O.V.E. and one that was going to restore the correct balance of power to the world and nothing, not even Darkdoom, was going to stop them. The Disciples' time had come and the world would be changed for ever.

'Assault team away,' a voice reported.

☻ ☻ ☻

'I've got something strange here, sir,' one of the Dreadnought's bridge crew reported.

'What is it?' Darkdoom asked, walking over to the man's station with Nero close behind.

'A large number of radar contacts directly above us, but they're tiny,' the man replied.

'It couldn't be a flock of birds, not at this altitude,' Darkdoom said as he studied the curious radar signature on the display. 'Some kind of weapons system?'

'It doesn't match any existing profile,' the crew member replied, 'but at their current rate of descent they will reach our altitude in forty-five seconds.'

Darkdoom frowned.

'Give me visual,' he ordered, turning towards a large display on the wall of the bridge. The screen lit up, relaying an image from one of the powerful high-definition cameras that were mounted on the Dreadnought's superstructure. At first it was almost impossible to see anything against the dark storm clouds, but then the camera zoomed in and Darkdoom could just make out a swarm of tiny black shapes.

'Whatever they are I don't like the look of them. Activate defensive-weapon systems,' Darkdoom ordered.

'Yes, sir,' another man responded from a nearby console. 'All defensive systems online. Trying to lock on to targets . . .'

'Report!' Darkdoom snapped after a few seconds had passed.

'Anti-missile batteries are online,' the man replied. 'Targets in range in three . . . two . . .'

Darkdoom watched in horror as suddenly each of the black blobs seemed to sprout a pair of wings and jet away in numerous different directions. Through the hull he could hear the distinctive buzzing sound of the heavy machine guns that formed the last line of anti-missile defence starting to open fire.

☢ ☢ ☢

A thousand feet above the Dreadnought the mercenary felt the air bladders in the G-suit he was wearing inflating, forcing the blood to his brain and ensuring that he would not pass out during any of the high-G manoeuvres that the flight pack strapped to his back was performing. He had no control over his own spiralling flight path; the systems in the pack were automatically steering him towards his designated target point on the Dreadnought while making sure that he was an almost impossible target for the huge vessel's defensive-weapon systems. He had to admit that he had felt a twinge of fear as they had plummeted in free fall towards the Dreadnought, but the flight pack had performed exactly as it had done during training. They had been preparing for this mission for weeks and at first it had taken some getting used to that sickening wrench as the winglets deployed and the jets fired, sending him spearing off on his own unique designated flight path, but he had to admit that he had grown to like the adrenalin rush. The flight pack banked hard to the left and dived, just as the air a few metres away was torn apart by bright white flashes of tracer-machine-gun fire. The mercenary breathed a sigh of relief. Furan had been honest with them: only about ninety per cent of them would make it to the Dreadnought, and that had been too close for comfort.

'ETA on target . . . ten seconds,' a soft synthetic voice said in his ear as the hull of the Dreadnought filled the view through his helmet visor. The jets fired again and he felt himself start to slow as he passed over the guard rail on the gantry running along the upper deck of the superstructure and landed gently on his feet just a couple of metres from a hatch that led inside. The winglets retracted and he quickly removed the bulky unit from his back. He hit a switch on the side of the smooth black pack and the cover retracted revealing an assault rifle and an equipment harness filled with spare ammunition clips and grenades. Behind him, another two of Furan's men landed on the gantry and began to remove their packs as he moved to the doorway and held a small silver box up to the locking mechanism. There was a short pause and then the door slid open with a hiss. The first mercenary looked over his shoulder and checked that his two companions were armed and ready. Seeing that they were, he went inside.

'Team Six, infiltration complete, proceeding with assault,' the mercenary said to the microphone inside his helmet.

'Roger that, Team Six,' a calm voice replied in his ear.

'Proceed on target. All targets beside primaries are expendable; repeat, expendable.'

'Understood,' the mercenary replied, raising his assault rifle and moving inside.

☻ ☻ ☻

'What's going on?' Otto asked Raven, as she followed him up the ramp into the Shroud. They could hear the sound of the Dreadnought's guns firing but they had no idea what they were firing at.

'Wait here,' Raven said to Otto and the others as she went back down the ramp and ran across the bay to where one of the ground crew was speaking frantically into his hand-held communicator. She spoke briefly to the man before hurrying back.

'Stay on board the Shroud. Lock the hatch and don't let anyone in but me, understood?' Raven said.

'What's happening?' Shelby asked quickly. 'Something's wrong, isn't it?'

'We're under attack,' Raven said matter of factly, pulling two long scabbards from among the equipment stowed on board. 'I'm going after Nero and Darkdoom.'

☻ ☻ ☻

'Hostile forces on multiple decks,' one of the Dreadnought's bridge crew reported.

55

'Where are the security teams?' Nero asked Darkdoom.

'There are none,' he replied, looking angry. 'They were due to come aboard tomorrow once the final technical checks were complete. We've been running with a skeleton crew to minimise the risks if anything should go wrong and I can only assume that whoever is responsible for this knew that.'

'We need to get you out of here,' Nero said calmly. 'We're outnumbered and out-gunned.'

'No, *you* have to go. Whoever has launched this attack cannot possibly know that you're here. Get my son out of here, Max. I will stay and fight.'

Nero looked like he might argue for a moment, but then he thought about his students who were now caught unexpectedly in the middle of this.

'Very well,' Nero said, 'but rest assured I will find whoever is responsible for this.' He place a hand on Darkdoom's shoulder.

'Of course you will,' Darkdoom replied with a grim smile, 'and I pity them when you do.'

With a nod Nero turned and hurried off the bridge. Darkdoom headed over to the security station, watching as the invading forces moved unmolested through the corridors of his ship.

'Incoming transmission, sir,' one of Darkdoom's crew reported. 'It's using a G.L.O.V.E. transmission protocol.'

'On screen,' Darkdoom replied quickly. The screen lit up, displaying the smiling face of Jason Drake.

'Drake, I should have known that I couldn't rely on you to crawl under a rock and die quietly somewhere,' Darkdoom said angrily.

'A pleasure to see you too, Diabolus,' Drake replied calmly. 'I believe it's time to discuss the terms of your surrender.'

'Now why would I do that?' Darkdoom snapped.

'Because I already have over a dozen strike teams on board your vessel whose standing orders are to execute anyone they encounter. The only way for you to prevent the bloodbath that is about to ensue is to surrender now. I'm only going to make this offer once. You will be captured or killed either way – it makes little difference to me.'

'Why, Drake? What makes you want to destroy everything we've spent so long building? G.L.O.V.E. was founded on the basis that individually we were weak but united we are strong . . .'

'United!' Drake spat angrily. 'Once we were united, but now things have changed. G.L.O.V.E. is no longer the organisation it was. People no longer fear us as they once did and that which people do not fear, they do not respect. Number One understood the importance of fear, the importance of rule through strength, and since we lost that leadership, we have lost our way. I will not sit idly by and watch as you lead this organisation down a road of compromise and weakness. I'm going to remind the world what it is to feel fear again and through that fear we will remain strong.'

'You sound like Number One,' Darkdoom said coldly. 'And we put him down like the rabid dog that he was. I swear that one day I'll do the same to you.'

'Enough!' Drake snapped. 'What is it to be? Surrender or massacre. The choice is yours.'

Darkdoom stared back at Drake. He could see it in his eyes, he was not bluffing. There was nothing to be gained by further resistance. It would just cost the lives of his crew.

'Power down the defence grid,' Darkdoom said quietly. 'All crew members are to surrender immediately.'

☻ ☻ ☻

Nero ducked into a corner behind a piece of heavy machinery as he heard the sound of approaching footsteps. A moment later three men wearing black military kit and carrying assault rifles rounded the corner ahead of him. They moved like professionals, sweeping the corridor slowly and carefully. It would only be a matter of seconds before they found him. Nero had always refused to carry a gun, much to Raven's displeasure, but even if he had been armed he would have stood no chance against three men with rifles. He would rather surrender with dignity than be found hiding like a trapped rat. He stepped out from his hiding place, hands raised, and the three black-clad men all raised their rifles, pointing them in his direction.

'Stay where you are,' the lead man barked. 'Down on your knees, hands on your head.'

The three men advanced as Nero dropped to his knees and put his hands on his head as instructed. The lead man lowered the muzzle of his rifle, pointing it at Nero's head, his finger tightening on the trigger. Just as he was about to fire a voice in his helmet spoke.

'New standing orders from command. All units are to capture and restrain any opposing forces; repeat, capture and restrain,' the voice said.

'Looks like Mr Drake doesn't want any more bodies,' the lead mercenary said, looking down at Nero. Nero felt a surge of anger at the mention of Drake's name. He had suspected that he would be planning some sort of attack on G.L.O.V.E. but he hadn't been expecting it to come as quickly as this. The soldier gestured for Nero to stand with an upwards twitch of his rifle's muzzle. 'I guess this is your lucky day,' the man said with a twisted smile.

'Happily, I can't say the same for you,' Nero said with a grim smile as he got to his feet.

The mercenary in the middle of the group of three

grunted with surprise, looking down at his chest where the tip of a blade crackling with purple energy had just appeared. He toppled forwards as Nero dived to one side. Raven stepped behind the second man and wrapped one arm around his throat while using her free hand to grab his rifle. As his finger jerked reflexively on the trigger she pulled the rifle hard, bringing it to bear on the other man, who staggered backwards, several rounds hitting him squarely in the chest. Finally she twisted the other man's head to one side with a sickening crunch and he fell life-lessly to the floor. She stepped forward and pulled her sword from the body of the first man to fall.

'Time to go,' she said, offering Nero her hand.

'Where are the others?' Nero asked quickly as he stood up.

'Waiting on board the Shroud,' Raven replied. 'Where's Diabolus?'

'On the bridge. He wouldn't come,' Nero replied.

'I'll get him,' Raven said, putting her katana back into one of the crossed scabbards on her back.

'No,' Nero said quickly. 'We have to get the students out of here. Especially Nigel. That mercenary just confirmed my suspicions: Jason Drake is behind this.'

Nero didn't want to think about what would happen if Drake got his hands on Darkdoom's son. Raven stared back down the corridor leading to the bridge, a look of angry frustration on her face. After a couple of seconds she let out a sigh and turned back towards Nero.

'You're right,' Raven said quietly. 'I just don't like leaving Diabolus behind like this. He's saved both our lives in the past.'

'And we will repay that favour,' Nero said firmly, 'but not today.'

Raven gave a small nod and picked up one of the dead men's rifles. Without another word, the pair of them hurried away down the corridor, heading for the hangar bay.

☢ ☢ ☢

'Well, that can't be good,' Otto whispered as their pilot was marched out of the control room by one of the soldiers who had been searching the area. The pilot had left the Shroud to see if he could find a way to initiate the ship's refuelling but had only managed to get himself captured in the process. Now Otto and the others lay hidden among the piles of equipment at one end of the passenger compartment, watching through the open loading hatch as the remaining soldiers began to methodically search the other two Shrouds docked in the hangar bay.

'Anyone got any ideas?' Shelby said quietly.

'Not really, unless you've got seven thermoptic camo

suits hidden somewhere that you're not telling us about,' Laura replied.

'I am thinking that the Arctic is not seeming like such a bad option now,' Franz said in a nervous whisper.

Otto's mind raced as he watched the two men move across the hangar towards them. He had only one option. Taking a deep breath he closed his eyes. Otto hadn't tried to connect directly to the digital world for months but he knew that his ability to directly interface with the computer systems that surrounded them might be their only chance. The noises of the world around him seemed to fade away and he had the uncanny sensation of detaching from his physical body. Suddenly the data network that kept the Dreadnought functioning appeared around him, a crystalline lattice pulsing with neon bursts of light. He extended his senses and searched for the control systems of the Shrouds in the hangar bay. They were protected by multiple layers of security and encryption, but Otto just brushed them aside as if they weren't there. He was surprised by the ease with which he'd been able to circumvent the protection; it was almost like someone else had done it for him. Suddenly he had an odd feeling that he was not alone, as if there was someone right behind him, and yet there was no one else there. He shook the sensation off and refocused on the task at hand. Finding the systems he wanted he seized control and allowed some of his consciousness to return to his body.

'Otto,' Wing whispered, placing his hand on his friend's shoulder, 'are you OK?'

'Fine,' Otto said, feeling the familiar sense of slight disorientation as he reconnected with the physical world. 'Keep your heads down.'

Otto pushed with his mind and the engines on one of the other Shrouds parked in the hangar bay whined into life. The two soldiers spun towards the unexpected noise, raising their rifles as the Shroud began to slowly lift off the deck. Both men opened fire, strafing the aircraft's cockpit with high velocity rounds, puncturing the fuselage and cracking the reinforced glass of the windows. The Shroud swivelled in mid-air, turning to face the startled mercenaries, and with a roar from the engines raced across the hangar straight towards them. One of the men dived out of the way but the other was hit full on by the rounded nose of the dropship, flying through the air and landing with a heavy thud several metres away. The other soldier climbed to his feet, raising his rifle again. Otto sent the Shroud spinning slowly on the spot, raising the nose and lowering the tail. The soldier just had time for one short burst of fire before the tail of the aircraft swung around, inches from the ground, and swatted him backwards with a bone-crunching smack.

'Get their guns,' Otto said quickly as he mentally

fought to control the spinning Shroud and bring it back down to the deck safely. Wing and Shelby ran from their hiding places, sprinting down the Shroud's loading ramp and towards the injured soldier's fallen weapons. The first man was almost on his feet when Wing reached him and put him down with a swift kick to the side of his head. Shelby scooped up the second soldier's rifle moments before he could reach it and levelled it at the advancing man.

'What are you going to do, little girl, shoot me?' the mercenary sneered as he stepped towards her. Shelby lowered the muzzle of the rifle and shot the thug in the knee. He dropped to the ground, howling in pain.

'Something like that, yeah,' Shelby replied, keeping the rifle levelled at the whimpering soldier.

Wing popped the clip out of the other soldier's rifle, smoothly removed the firing pin and threw it across the hangar, dropping the useless gun to the floor with a look of distaste. Otto shut down the engines on the Shroud that he had been controlling and followed Laura and the others over to where Shelby and Wing were standing.

'Jeez,' Lucy said, looking down at the wounded man, 'you guys weren't kidding about the whole trouble magnets thing, were you?'

Wing stepped forward and placed one foot on the soldier's wounded knee.

'I have no desire to inflict further pain on you,' he said calmly, 'but I will if you force me to. How many more of you are there?'

'More than you can handle,' the soldier spat angrily.

'How many?' Wing repeated, pressing his foot down slightly.

'Aaargh,' the man cried out in pain. 'OK, OK . . . at least thirty, maybe more.'

'Thank you,' Wing said, taking his foot off the soldier's injured leg, 'you've been most helpful.'

Wing reached down and pinched a point at the side of the man's neck and his eyes rolled upwards as he collapsed backwards, unconscious.

'OK,' Otto said quickly, 'we have to get out of here. It's safe to assume that it won't be long before they send another team to check on these guys and I, for one, would rather not be here when they do.'

'Agreed,' Laura said, 'but that's easier said than done. Even if we can get the hangar door open, none of us can fly one of these things.'

'Which means we have to wait for Raven to get back here with Nero and my dad,' Nigel said.

There was the sound of gunfire from the other side of the hangar as Raven and Nero sprinted through the door.

'To be speaking of the devils,' Franz said nervously.

'Where's my dad?' Nigel said half to himself.

Raven stopped and raised the rifle she was carrying to her shoulder, firing a short burst through the door behind her. Nero ran towards his students and grabbed the rifle from Shelby.

'Get to the Shroud, NOW!' Nero barked, turning to squeeze off a burst of cover fire as Raven sprinted across the hangar towards them. Three soldiers ran through the doorway from where Nero and Raven had just come and returned fire, rounds buzzing past Otto and the others like angry hornets as they boarded the Shroud. Raven and Nero continued to return fire and Raven pulled a small grey cylinder from her belt, lobbing it towards the soldiers coming from the doorway. There was a flash and a loud bang and the area began to fill with thick white smoke.

Raven and Nero took advantage of the temporary diversion and were only a few metres from the ramp when there was another short burst of fire from somewhere behind them. Raven grunted, staggering forwards as a bullet hit her in the thigh. Nero caught her before she could fall to the ground and helped her up the last few steps of the Shroud's loading ramp. He smacked the large red button on the bulkhead to raise the ramp and lowered Raven gently to the ground. He ran towards the front of the passenger compartment, ripped an emergency medical kit from its mount on the wall and threw it to Wing.

'Gauze pads, apply pressure to the wound,' Nero said angrily, pointing at Raven. 'Malpense, with me!'

Nero climbed quickly up the ladder to the flight deck with Otto right behind him as Wing tore the medical kit open. Nero collapsed into the pilot's seat and punched a series of buttons on the consoles surrounding him.

'Get those doors open,' Nero snapped at Otto, pointing at the heavy steel slabs that sealed the hangar. Otto didn't hesitate for a second; he just closed his eyes and reached out once again for the Dreadnought's control systems. What could only have been a couple of seconds seemed like hours as he frantically searched through the hangar sections sub-routines looking for the door controls.

Down in the passenger compartment, Wing pressed a pad against the bullet wounds in Raven's thigh, the gauze already soaked with blood. Raven inhaled sharply, putting her hand on top of Wing's and pressing down more firmly as more rounds hit the Shroud's hull outside as it lifted off.

Up on the flight deck, Nero pulled at the joystick and turned the hovering Shroud towards the hangar doors.

'Otto . . .' Nero said impatiently.

'Got it!' he yelled, his eyes flying open to see the huge steel doors begin to slide apart. Nero waited for a couple of seconds as the doors ground open and then pushed hard on the throttle control. Otto grabbed for a handhold on the back of Nero's seat as the Shroud shot forwards and through the widening gap with only centimetres to spare.

☻☻☻

In the control room aboard the cloaked aircraft high above the Dreadnought, Jason Drake slammed his fist down on the radar console in front of him. He watched the replay of the video feed from the camera mounted on the helmet of one of his men in the hangar. There was no doubt about it: the two figures running across the hangar just before they were obscured by a cloud of dense white smoke were Nero and his pet assassin, Raven.

'Contact the Dreadnought. Have them blow that Shroud out of the sky!' he yelled angrily. Drake knew that his own aircraft was too large and too slow to give chase.

'Our men have only just taken the bridge, sir,' one of Drake's men replied nervously. 'We won't have access to the weapons systems for a few more minutes.'

Drake cursed quietly to himself. 'Retask satellites nine and thirteen, track its flight path and scramble an intercept team to go in as soon as we've worked out where it's going to land,' Drake ordered. 'There are to be no survivors, understood?'

'Yes, sir.'

chapter four

Nero scanned the Shroud's control panel with a worried expression. They were low on fuel. He knew that he was going to have to put the Shroud down somewhere very soon. They had no chance of making it back to H.I.V.E.; their best chance was if he could touch down somewhere near one of the safe houses that Raven maintained for just such an occasion in various cities around the world. He plotted their flight range against their remaining fuel load and realised that there was only one realistic option, but it would mean flying through some of the most densely populated airspace on the planet. He punched the destination coordinates into the autopilot and activated it. He knew that the Shroud's stealth systems would render it undetectable to civilian or military radar, but he also knew the increased power consumption would mean running out of fuel while they were still over the ocean – clearly not a desirable outcome. So he had to work on the assumption that wherever they went, Drake would be able to follow them. He got up out of the pilot's seat and climbed down the ladder to the passenger compartment. Raven sat applying a field dressing to her leg in one of the seats that ran along the side of the compartment.

'How is it?' Nero asked as he sat down beside her.

'The bullet went straight through,' she said, pulling the plastic cap from a syringe with her teeth and sticking it into her leg just above the wound. 'I've had far worse, as you well know.'

'Indeed,' Nero said with a slight smile. 'I'm taking us to one of your safe houses. I assume you have all the medical supplies you'll need there.'

'Of course,' Raven replied, leaning back against the bulkhead. 'Have you contacted anyone else yet to let them know what has happened?'

'No, not yet,' Nero replied. 'I'll contact H.I.V.E. once we reach the safe house. To be honest I don't know who else we can trust at the moment.'

'Hardly an unusual state of affairs in our line of work,' Raven replied.

On the other side of the compartment Otto sat watching Nero and Raven's hushed conversation. Nero had said nothing to them about what had happened on the Dreadnought or who was responsible, but he could tell from their expressions that something had gone very wrong.

'I guess we can forget the training mission then,' Laura said quietly, sitting down next to Otto.

'Looks that way,' Otto said, rubbing his temples with a frown.

'Something wrong?' Laura asked.

'I don't know,' Otto said quietly.

'What do you mean?' Laura asked, looking worried.

'It's probably nothing,' Otto said. 'It's just that when I took control of that Shroud I felt something weird.'

'Weird how?' Laura said.

'Weird like there was someone helping me,' Otto said, staring at the floor. 'It's hard to describe, but it's not the first time I've felt it. It's like there's someone with me, giving me their strength.'

'It's happened before?' Laura asked.

'Yeah,' Otto replied, 'like I say, it's hard to explain. I'm not sure I like it much. It feels as though I'm sharing my head with someone.'

'I wouldn't worry about it,' Laura said, putting her hand on Otto's knee. 'This thing you can do is strange enough as it is, it's hardly surprising that sometimes you find it hard to understand everything that's going on. You're interfacing with machines while in an altered state of consciousness – that's got to register pretty high on the weird scale. Who knows what tricks that brain of yours could be playing on you?'

'I suppose you're right,' Otto said with a sigh. 'I just hope I'm not losing it.'

'Even if you are, who's honestly going to notice one more nutcase in this asylum?' Laura said with a grin, gesturing at the others sitting around the compartment.

'Well, there is that I guess,' Otto said with a smile.

☻ ☻ ☻

The Shroud descended towards the skyline of New York City as the first light of dawn began to spread across the city. Nero glanced at the fuel readouts. He'd had no choice but to engage the Shroud's thermoptic camouflage system as they flew into one of the most densely populated areas on Earth, but that meant the tiny amount of fuel remaining was disappearing at an alarming rate. He steered towards the coordinates of Raven's safe house, hoping quietly to himself that he could find somewhere discreet enough to land nearby. He flew low over the warehouse buildings and industrial units that were dotted close to the river. The fact that it was so early in the morning meant there were fewer people and cars on the streets, but there were still enough witnesses around to make an uncloaked landing impossible. This was, after all, the city that never sleeps, Nero thought to himself.

The Shroud was now more or less on top of the correct coordinates and Nero spotted what looked like a viable spot to land in the middle of a loading area behind an abandoned warehouse. He dropped the Shroud gently on to the asphalt with barely a bump – only the faintest whisper of engine noise and a rush of wind from the engines' downwash gave away the fact that they were there at all. Nero breathed a sigh of relief and climbed out of the pilot's seat, hurrying down the ladder that led below.

'We must move quickly,' he instructed as Raven ushered the students towards the loading ramp that was slowly descending at the rear of the compartment. Nero watched Raven and the others move away from the Shroud and then climbed quickly back up to the flight deck and punched a series of commands into the autopilot. He checked the instructions just once before hurrying back down the ladder to join the others as the loading ramp closed behind him, and with a rush of wind and an almost inaudible whine the Shroud lifted off again. With luck, if the fuel held out, it would crash into the sea offshore in a few minutes' time. They could not afford to leave it uncloaked when the fuel ran out. A military-grade aircraft of unknown design being found in the middle of New York would draw far too much unwanted attention, even if its passengers and crew were long gone.

'Are you OK to walk?' Nero asked Raven.

'Fine. Let's go,' Raven said, pushing herself away from

the wall she had been leaning against. Nero and the others followed as she made her way to the gate leading out of the loading area, only limping slightly. She gestured for them all to stay put while she checked the pavement on the other side of the gate. There were a couple of people walking down the road and the odd car trundling past. Raven ducked back inside.

'The safe house is not far, about a block east of here,' she said quietly, 'but we are not the most inconspicuous group.' Raven gestured at the students' black uniform jumpsuits. 'So we need to move quickly and attract as little attention to ourselves as possible.'

Without any further delay she stepped through the gate and the others followed. They moved quickly along the street, drawing a couple of curious looks from passers-by but no more than that. Soon they arrived at a flight of stairs that led down from the pavement to an old, battered wooden door in the basement of the building above. Raven limped down the steps and pulled a single loose brick from the wall beside the doorway. Behind it was a small numeric keypad into which she punched a short series of digits. With a mechanical clunk the door swung open.

As Otto passed through he noticed that the old wooden door was actually a heavy armour-plated panel that was merely dressed with an old wooden façade on the outside.

Raven hit a switch near the door and fluorescent lights flickered on, revealing a large open room that was lined with equipment lockers and other items draped with dust sheets. Judging by the stale smell of the air, the room had been empty for quite some time.

'Make yourselves at home,' Raven said, gesturing at the room around them, 'just don't touch anything till I've disabled the booby traps.'

The students all stopped moving and looked nervously around the room.

'Oh, don't worry,' Raven said with a grim smile. 'They're non-lethal . . . mostly.'

Otto and the others stood still while Raven and Nero moved around the room, pulling the dust covers off the equipment that surrounded them.

'Booby traps?' Nero whispered once they were on the other side of the room, raising a single eyebrow.

'Of course not,' Raven said, smiling. 'Worked though, didn't it?' She nodded over her shoulder to where the group of slightly nervous-looking Alphas were all standing very still.

Nero and Raven finished uncovering the equipment and brought four chairs that had been positioned at the workstations over to the pair of camp beds that sat against the wall in one corner. Nero beckoned his students over and gestured for them to sit.

'Not very comfortable, I'm afraid,' Nero said as the Alphas sat down on the chairs and beds, 'but hopefully we won't be here for long.'

'Doctor Nero,' Laura said nervously, 'can you tell us what happened on board the Dreadnought?'

'Something very unfortunate,' Nero said with a sigh, 'but rest assured that we intend to rectify the situation as soon as possible.'

'What happened to my dad?' Nigel asked quietly.

'He was captured,' Nero said, placing a hand on Nigel's shoulder, 'but we *will* get him back. Our first priority, though, is returning you all safely to H.I.V.E.'

'Isn't there anything we can do to help?' Otto asked quickly.

'While I appreciate your enthusiasm, Mr Malpense, and I do of course respect your unique talents, this is a job for more *experienced* operatives,' Nero replied carefully.

'With respect, Doctor Nero,' Wing said calmly, 'is this not exactly the type of experience that we might require in the future?'

Nero smiled, despite himself. 'I think this particular group has more than adequate familiarity with life-threatening situations, Mr Fanchu,' he replied.

Nero could not help but feel a twinge of pride as he looked at the determined young faces that stared back at him. They would all make admirable G.L.O.V.E. operatives in the future, but they were not yet well trained enough to take on the sort of mission that Nero was anticipating would be necessary to retrieve Darkdoom and eliminate Drake and his allies.

'Besides,' Nero said with a crooked smile, 'you all have an appointment to keep in the Arctic, I believe.'

There were a couple of groans as Nero turned and walked back over to where Raven was tapping away at a keyboard. The only upside to the events of earlier that day had been that they seemed likely to get them out of the Arctic survival course.

'Why won't they let us help?' Nigel whispered, frowning as Nero walked away.

'We *have* handled this kind of thing before,' Shelby said, looking indignant.

'Erm . . . not all of us,' Lucy said with a nervous smile. 'Wouldn't we be better off leaving this to the specialists?'

'I am agreeing,' Franz said quietly. 'I am thinking that I do not like being shot at very much.'

'You wouldn't say that if it was *your* dad!' Nigel snapped at Franz.

'Guys!' Otto said quickly. 'Come on, we're all friends here. Nigel, I know you're worried but perhaps Lucy and Franz are right. We may all think we know what we're doing, but G.L.O.V.E. must have people better trained for this sort of thing than us. We might be able to get on board the Dreadnought, sure, but armed hostage retrieval, that's another matter. Besides, do you really think your dad would want you putting your life at risk again to save his?'

'I suppose not,' Nigel said quietly, 'but I hate just sitting around like this when God knows what could be happening to him.'

Franz put his hand on Nigel's shoulder. 'They'll get him back,' he said, 'don't be worrying.'

'Easier said than done,' Nigel sighed, staring sadly at the floor.

'Any problems?' Raven asked as Nero walked over to her.

'I suspect the only problem we're going to have is ensuring they don't stage an assault on Drake's location themselves,' Nero replied, glancing over at the students.

'Speaking of which,' Raven said, pulling up a satellite overview map on the screen in front of her, 'this is the last known location of the Dreadnought.' She pointed at an area of the map. 'My bet is that they'll bring her down somewhere. They know we'll be searching for them and while it can be hidden from most observers, we know exactly what we're looking for.'

'We can track the storm,' Nero said, looking more closely at the satellite imagery.

'Exactly,' Raven replied. 'This is two hours ago.' She

pulled up another image on the screen. 'You can see the Dreadnought's storm cloak here, but then an hour ago it disappeared.'

'They switched to thermoptic camouflage,' Nero said, frustration clear in his voice.

'It would appear so,' Raven replied. 'But they can't keep the cloak up indefinitely – it would place too much strain on their power core keeping something that big cloaked permanently. That's probably why they have the storm generator, so they can conceal her without the massive power drain.'

'So they need somewhere to hide,' Nero said, 'but where? The Dreadnought is designed to stay airborne indefinitely. It's not able to just land wherever it chooses.'

'No, there has to be a maintenance facility somewhere,' Raven continued, 'a kind of dry dock, somewhere that repairs could be made if necessary. Probably the same facility it was constructed at.'

'Which is where?' Nero asked.

'That, as they say, is the million-dollar question,' Raven replied. 'All data on the Dreadnought, including all details of its construction, have been erased from G.L.O.V.E.'s central database.'

'Drake's doing, no doubt,' Nero said.

'No doubt,' Raven replied. 'But that doesn't mean there is no record anywhere. Drake Industries may have built the thing in secret but it would be hard, if not impossible, to keep all records of a project on that scale completely buried.'

'So we have to get their records,' Nero said quietly. 'Can they be accessed remotely?'

'Unlikely, but their head office is here in New York,' Raven replied. 'If we can get into their servers we may be able to find out where the Dreadnought was built and, therefore, where, in all likelihood, it is being hidden.'

'We need to put together an infiltration team,' Nero said quickly. 'We have to get that location as quickly as possible.'

'Shall I contact the ruling council?' Raven asked.

Nero was silent for a moment, running through all the different scenarios in his head.

'No,' he said after a few seconds. 'Putting together a G.L.O.V.E. team will take too long and I'm still not sure that everyone on the council can be trusted. Besides which, I fear that Diabolus's current life expectancy could be measured in hours rather than days.'

'That's if he's even still alive,' Raven whispered.

'We have to work on the assumption that he is, for now at least,' Nero replied quietly, glancing over at Nigel, who sat in silence as his friends chatted quietly among themselves. 'We need to do this now and, while I wish there was another way, we do have everyone we need to get inside Drake's network right here. Whether we like it or not.'

'Otto,' Raven whispered.

'Exactly,' Nero replied quietly.

'I'll try and get the schematics of the Drake Industries building, see if I can find a way to get Malpense and myself into it undetected,' Raven said, turning back towards the workstation.

'No, you need to rest,' Nero said quietly. 'That wound in your leg may not be too bad, but you're still not in a fit state for that. I'll take him myself and we won't be needing any building schematics because we're going to walk straight through the front door. If Jason Drake thinks he can force me to go crawling through sewers or ventilation ducts then he has another think coming. Anyway, someone has to stay here and keep an eye on the rest of our charges.' Nero gestured to the students sat at the other end of the room.

'Are you sure?' Raven asked, looking worried.

'Of course,' Nero replied. 'I may concentrate on running H.I.V.E. these days but I haven't completely lost my edge, you know.'

'I wouldn't dream of suggesting you had,' Raven said with a slight smile. 'You might want to take Fanchu with you as well, though. You'll need someone to watch your back.'

'Very well,' Nero replied. 'I'll have to find some less conspicuous clothing for them. I assume you have some pocket money lying around here somewhere?'

Raven limped over to a safe that was mounted on the wall and punched a combination into the digital keypad. The lock disengaged with a thunk and Raven opened it to reveal large piles of money in each of the world's most significant currencies. She picked up a stack of US dollars and tossed them to Nero.

'Don't spend it all at once.'

'You're too kind,' Nero said, tucking the money inside his jacket. 'I shouldn't be long. While I'm gone, try and contact H.I.V.E. See how long it would take them to get a Shroud here to pick us up. Only tell them we're in New York though – don't give them our precise location. Better to err on the side of caution at this point.'

'Understood,' Raven replied. 'I'll put together some equipment for you.'

Nero nodded and headed out of the door and on to the street.

☠ ☠ ☠

The rattlesnake slithered under the nearest rock as the desert floor began to shake. With a rumble a crack appeared in the scorched wasteland and slowly began to widen. Before long a giant rectangular hole in the desert had opened and after a couple more seconds it was illuminated by an array of landing lights. Clouds of dust were kicked up as a strange wind seemed to materialise from nowhere, accompanied by a low throbbing roar.

The cloaked Dreadnought descended into the cavernous underground hangar as huge supporting arms slid out from the walls and connected to hard-points on the massive vessel's hull. The hangar doors slowly rumbled closed again and with a sharp electrical crackle the thermoptic cloaking field disengaged. Large robotic arms swung out and began to attach umbilical cables and hoses to the Dreadnought as a gantry extended and connected to the external hatchway on the bridge. The hatch hissed open and Jason Drake stepped out on to the narrow walkway. A tall, heavily muscled man with closely shaved grey hair and a star-shaped pattern of scars that surrounded his blind right eye offered his hand to Drake.

'Congratulations,' the man said with a grim smile, 'and welcome home.' He had a thick Ukrainian accent.

'Thank you, Pietor,' Drake replied, 'though it is your men that should really be congratulated. Their performance was exemplary.'

'I would expect nothing less,' Furan said. 'I only employ the best and the punishments for failure are terminal. Such penalties and large sums of money tend to act as good motivators. The carrot and the stick, as they say. You have Darkdoom?'

'Yes, he's in the Dreadnought's brig. I've ordered a security team to transfer him to the holding cells until we're ready for phase two.'

'I was not sure you would take him alive,' Furan remarked as they made their way down the walkway.

'Nor was I,' Drake said, 'but the fact that we did just emphasises his weakness. You or I would never have let ourselves be captured like that. The man has no spine. Nero though is quite another matter. We have to find him before he can warn the rest of G.L.O.V.E. what's going on.'

'It's too late for them to stop us now,' Furan replied. 'We have everything we need. There's nothing Nero can do.'

'Don't underestimate,' Drake warned him, frowning. 'That's the mistake Number One made and it cost him his life. Do we have anything from Overwatch yet?'

'No, they engaged their cloak en route to New York. They're scanning the area but it will take time. The rest of the Disciples are keen to know of our progress. They have requested that you report in.'

'Very well, I will contact them shortly,' Drake replied as a man wearing a desert camouflage uniform came running up the walkway towards them. He saluted Furan and Drake smartly.

'Sir, Overwatch has something,' the man said quickly. 'I think we've found them.'

☻ ☻ ☻

'We can have two Shrouds with you in about ten hours. I wish it could be sooner but you're a long way from home,' Colonel Francisco said as Chief Monroe, the head of H.I.V.E. security, joined him at the screen. They stood in H.I.V.E.'s security control centre, which was now bustling with frantic activity as the department worked to put together a retrieval team for Nero, Raven and the others. Monroe had given Francisco his best men. It would leave H.I.V.E. lightly defended until they returned, but it was a chance they would have to take.

'The teams are on their way to the hangar now,' the Chief said. 'They'll be ready for wheels-up in three minutes.'

'You'd be better off contacting G.L.O.V.E. command and getting a pick-up from a local team,' Francisco said, frowning. 'They could be with you much more quickly.'

'No,' Raven said, her face filling the screen on the console in front of them. 'Nero wants to keep this in-house. He's not sure who we can trust at the moment and if we use a G.L.O.V.E. team we can't be sure that they'll be the only ones who are given our location.'

'We don't have your precise location yet,' Monroe said, looking unhappy.

'I know, Chief. It's not that we can't trust you or the Colonel, but the later we leave giving you that information the less likely it is to end up in the wrong hands,' Raven replied. 'I'll transmit the pick-up coordinates to you when the Shroud is fifteen kilometres out. That way, even if the transmission is intercepted, it will be too late for anyone to move on our location.'

'Understood. Where's Nero?' Francisco asked.

'Would you believe me if I told you he'd gone shopping?' Raven asked with a smile.

'I don't want to know,' Francisco said, shaking his head. 'I'll contact you on this channel when we're within range of your position.'

☹ ☹ ☹

'How are you liking your first field trip then?' Otto asked, sitting down on the camp bed next to Lucy. Shelby and Laura were busy trying to teach Wing how to play poker with a pack of cards that Raven had found, while Franz sat chatting away happily to Nigel, who looked like he just wanted some peace and quiet.

'Never been shot at before,' Lucy replied with a worried smile. 'Just another first to add to the list from the past couple of days.'

'You mind me asking something?' Otto said.

'No, go ahead.'

'How did you end up here?'

'I told you, I got *invited* by our friend over there.' Lucy jerked her thumb at Raven, who was gathering equipment from the lockers around the room.

'No, I mean, what did you do to deserve this?' Otto said with a smile.

'What do you mean?' Lucy replied, frowning slightly.

'Well, we're all here – well, not here in this basement, but at H.I.V.E. – for a reason,' Otto said. 'Shelby, Laura, me . . . we have what you could call talents, things that might make us useful to G.L.O.V.E. in the future. Nigel, Franz and Wing, on the other hand, got sent to the school by their parents or they had family ties to G.L.O.V.E. though they didn't all know that when they first arrived. Now, you can tell me to mind my own business if you want, but I'm just curious how you ended up being stuck with us lot.'

'Honestly?' Lucy said. 'I have no idea. As far as I know there are no super-villains in the family and I don't have any special abilities that anyone might find useful. If there's a reason for me to be here, I don't know what it is.'

Otto liked to think that he could tell when someone was lying and Lucy seemed to be being completely truthful. He could only imagine what it must be like for her to be taken from what sounded like a quite normal existence and thrust into their world with no idea of what it was that marked her out as a G.L.O.V.E. operative of the future. The fact that she'd been put into the Alpha stream meant that there had to be considerable potential that Lucy had or part of her history that G.L.O.V.E. knew about but that she didn't understand. Not yet, at least.

'That must, to use a technical term, suck,' he said with a slight smile.

'Big time,' Lucy responded with a grin. 'I will say this for life at H.I.V.E. though, it's certainly not boring.'

'That much is true. Unpredictable, dangerous, potentially lethal even, but never boring.'

'You have any idea what was going on back at the Dreadnought?' Lucy asked. 'Like, who those guys were and why they were shooting at us? Doctor Nero didn't really tell us anything.'

'I honestly have no idea,' Otto replied with a sigh. 'Never quite knowing exactly why people want you dead is pretty much par for the course around here, I'm afraid.'

'Just something else I'm going to have to get used to then.' She smiled at Otto. 'You know, I really appreciate the way you guys have been letting me tag along and explaining how things work around here.'

'It's the least we can do,' Otto said. 'We all remember what it was like when we first arrived at H.I.V.E. It's a bit like being dropped into a tank full of sharks while you've got a nosebleed.'

'That's one way of putting it,' Lucy laughed, putting her hand on Otto's knee, 'but seriously, thanks, you've been really kind.'

'Hey, are you two going to come and join in?' Laura called, gesturing at the cards that lay on the table in front of her, Wing and Shelby. Otto thought he had seen her frown for a moment, but it had vanished now and was replaced by a friendly smile.

'Yeah and a big thank you to whoever thought it was a good idea to teach Wing how to play,' Shelby said with a grin, 'the guy with the natural poker face. We could do with some help. He's cleaning us out here.'

'I have a poker face?' Wing asked, raising a quizzical eyebrow. 'I thought you were just really, really bad at this game.'

'Oh, you are so going down now, karate kid,' Shelby said, punching Wing in the shoulder.

There was a sudden clunking sound as the safe-house door unlocked and Nero walked in carrying several large bags. He placed them on a table and turned to face his assembled students.

'Mr Malpense, Mr Fanchu, a moment of your time please.' Nero gestured for them to follow him as he walked back across the room to where Raven was waiting. Various pieces of equipment were arranged in front of her, some of which Otto recognised, but there were others he had never seen before.

'I require your assistance, gentlemen,' Nero said, a serious look on his face. 'I'm sure you both already appreciate that it is imperative we discover the location of the Dreadnought if we're to regain control of it and rescue Diabolus. Raven and myself believe we have come up with a way to retrieve that information. The assault on the Dreadnought was masterminded by a man called Jason Drake. You may well have heard of him before now as the CEO of Drake Industries, but what you won't have been aware of is that he has been a senior member of the G.L.O.V.E. ruling council for some time. Recently he has left his position on the council and now seems intent on destroying the organisation he once served. His motivations are unclear, beyond the fact that he did not believe we should have acted against Number One in the way we did.'

'But Number One was Overlord,' Otto said, frowning. 'Surely he doesn't believe that psychotic thing should have been allowed to carry out its plans. Drake would have been just as dead as the rest of us if Overlord had got its way.'

'Unfortunately the only people who witnessed what happened on Overlord's satellite are you and me, Mr

Malpense. There are some on the ruling council, Drake especially, who have always been sceptical about our account of events. They believe we merely concocted a story to excuse a coup d'état, that in reality we were just making a ruthless grab for control of G.L.O.V.E. Unfortunately we have no hard evidence to prove that our version of what happened is a true account of events that day and Drake is taking advantage of that fact.'

'So what do we need to do?' Wing asked calmly.

'The global headquarters of Drake Industries is here in New York, and I believe that if we can get access to their central mainframe that you, Mr Malpense, might be able to acquire the location of wherever the Dreadnought is being hidden.'

'Surely it's unlikely that Drake would keep that information on the network of his legitimate front company?' Otto asked.

'Of course,' Nero replied, 'but if the Dreadnought is being concealed at the installation where it was built, or at some other hidden location, there may be some evidence of the construction of that facility hidden on their servers,' Nero explained. 'I know from my own past experience with the construction of H.I.V.E. that it's almost impossible to keep all records of such a project completely disguised.'

'Ghost data,' Otto said.

'Exactly,' Raven replied. 'If we – or more specifically you, Otto – can put those traces together, it's conceivable that we can discover where Darkdoom is being held. You are the only person who can do that quickly enough. We have to stop Drake now.'

'Indeed,' Nero agreed. 'It is highly unlikely that the assault on the Dreadnought was Drake's endgame. I'm sure he's planning something else, which would unfortunately mean that this is just the beginning.'

'So how are we going to do this?' Otto asked.

'We're taking the direct approach,' Nero said, gesturing at the equipment that lay arranged on the table.

chapter five

Drake strode into the control centre of the underground facility and made straight for the giant high-definition tabletop display screen in the middle of the room. He stared down at the surface that was currently displaying an incredibly detailed real-time satellite view of the majority of New York's metropolitan area.

'Where are they?' he asked, scanning the display.

'We picked Nero up here,' Furan said, pointing at an area of central Manhattan. As he touched the glass surface of the display it zoomed in and a smaller window popped up showing a man walking through the front door of one of the shops that lined the street they were looking at.

'You're sure it's Nero?' Drake asked. From this overhead angle it was impossible to make out any details of the man's face.

Furan pressed one of the interface controls at the edge

of the display and the image of the man walking into the shop zoomed in still further. A wireframe overlay appeared on the long shadow that the man cast on the sidewalk, capturing the shape of his profile over the course of several seconds. These silhouettes were then overlaid on a pre-existing image of Nero's face and reference points were matched up. The whole process took only a matter of seconds before a box appeared reading 'Match Probability: 93.8%'.

Drake smiled. The system had cost billions to develop for the US government but the investment had been worthwhile. Overwatch was the most sophisticated surveillance system that had ever been built and it gave the US government the unique ability to quickly track down a single man in a city of over twenty million people. Of course, what the government did not know was that Drake had built his own back door into the system that gave him total covert control of the watchful satellites orbiting far overhead. Not only could he find anyone he wanted almost anywhere on the planet but he could also ensure that the government never found anyone that Drake wanted to remain hidden. It was the best of both worlds.

'With a match probability that high I think it's safe to say that's him,' Furan said.

'Where did he go after this?' Drake asked.

'We tracked him to this location on the other side of the river,' Furan replied, pulling up an image of Nero walking into the basement of a nondescript apartment building.

'And he's still there?'

'Yes, he's been inside for the past ten minutes.'

'Excellent.' Drake smiled. 'Dispatch a retrieval team. Make sure they are fully prepared. Raven's in there with him, remember.'

'Of course.' Furan nodded. 'I shall send my best men.'

☻ ☻ ☻

Otto looked at himself in the small mirror on the wall of the safe house's small bathroom. He had changed into the clothes that Nero had bought for him and been surprised by just how weird they felt. He had become very used to wearing his familiar Alpha jumpsuit and now, as he stood there in jeans and a long-sleeved black top, he couldn't decide if he actually liked it or not.

He ran his fingers through the mess of spiky white hair on his head. He'd never really thought about this most obvious physical side effect of the cloning technique that had given him life, but he knew that it marked him out as something strange or different and he wasn't sure any more if that was something he wanted to be. He'd been created as a new body for someone else, constructed instead of naturally born, and the full realisation of that fact had left him feeling slightly alienated from the people around him. The only people who knew the truth of his origins were Nero and himself, and while he had debated telling his friends what he had learnt about his creation, something had stopped him. He hadn't even told Wing.

The other significant consequence of his encounter with Overlord was that he was becoming increasingly reluctant to use his ability to interface directly with computers and other electronic devices. It just seemed to remind him of how he himself was closer to *being* a machine than the others, just a manufactured item, a tool.

Unfortunately, Nero's plan called for him to use exactly those abilities and, under the circumstances, there was no way he could refuse. Otto took a deep breath and let it out slowly. Standing there brooding about these things wasn't going to help anyone. He opened the door and walked out into the main room, throwing his H.I.V.E. uniform on to the table next to Wing's. Wing smiled at him as he walked over.

'Does this feel as weird to you as it does to me?' Wing asked.

'Yup,' Otto said with a grin. 'I never thought I'd actually miss wearing a jumpsuit.'

'You know, you two *almost* look normal,' Laura said as Otto and Wing joined the others.

'Thanks . . . I think,' Otto replied, raising an eyebrow.

'Ja, you are looking like the real people,' Franz said happily.

'*I* want some new clothes,' Shelby said with mock indignation. 'I can't believe I've been wearing the same thing for this long. Back home I used to be a three-outfits-a-day girl. I thought that villains were supposed to get the best outfits, not the most boring and practical ones.'

'I quite like not having to worry about what I'm going to wear,' Nigel said, 'but I can see how a H.I.V.E. uniform might look a little bit odd out on the street.'

'So, you guys gonna be long?' Shelby asked.

'Shouldn't be,' Otto replied, 'if everything goes according to plan we should be straight in and out.'

'Like that's going to happen,' Laura said, grinning. 'Since when do things go according to plan for us?'

'There is nothing more boring than a predictable outcome,' Wing commented with a slight smile.

'Hey, I like boring and predictable,' Otto said quickly. 'It's less likely to end in, you know . . . pain, death, all that stuff. We need more boring and predictable in our lives.'

'Are you two ready?' Nero asked from the other side of the room, where he was busy packing pieces of equipment into two identical black backpacks.

'I think so,' Otto said, glancing at Wing, who gave a tiny nod.

'Good, we should leave,' Nero continued as he zipped up one of the backpacks and held it out for Otto. 'You are clear on the plan?'

'Yes,' Otto replied, taking the bag.

'Be careful,' Raven said, picking up the second bag and handing it to Wing. 'This may be a civilian facility but security will be tight. Be prepared to improvise.'

'Time to go,' Nero said and gestured for the two boys to follow him as he headed for the door.

☢ ☢ ☢

'Nero and two others are leaving the building,' one of Drake's operatives reported, turning away from the screen he had been monitoring. Drake quickly walked over to the man's station and examined the display.

'Who's that with him?' Drake asked. The man at the console punched in a series of commands and far above them in orbit the cameras of one of the Overwatch satellites obeyed, zooming in and refocusing on the three tiny figures in the centre of the screen. The system began to perform the same calculations that it had used to identify Nero, trying to attach names to the two anonymous figures who now accompanied him. Only a few seconds passed and then two profiles popped up on screen next to each other.

'Otto Malpense and Wing Fanchu,' Drake said quietly

as he read the information. He was not familiar with either of them but it was clear from the G.L.O.V.E. records that they were both students at H.I.V.E. Where was Nero going with them, and why wasn't Raven there too?

'They're heading for the subway, sir,' the operative reported, just as Nero and his companions disappeared down the stairs leading into one of the numerous underground stations throughout the city. 'We can't track them in there.'

'I'm quite aware of that,' Drake snapped at the man. Overwatch was capable of many things but it could not see beneath the ground. He doubted that Nero had any idea he was being tracked, but even if he had he could not have chosen a better way to evade detection. 'Monitor all exits from the subway system. I want to know the moment they resurface.'

'But, sir, there are over four hundred stations in the city,' the man replied. 'Monitoring them all is nearly impossible. With the number of passengers coming and going, even Overwatch can't hope to sort through that many people.'

'I don't care how hard it is!' Drake yelled angrily. 'Just find him or he won't be the only one underground, do I make myself clear?'

'Yes, sir,' the man said, swallowing nervously.

'How far out is the retrieval team?' Drake asked, turning to Furan.

'Just under an hour,' Furan said, checking his watch.

'And the hunter drones?' Drake asked.

'The launch vehicle is in position and awaiting targets,' Furan replied.

Drake nodded and a slight smile flickered across his face. He had wanted to capture Nero intact, but if push came to shove at least he could make sure that he would never leave New York City alive.

☮ ☮ ☮

Nero walked up the stairs leading to the street above. The city was properly awake now and the streets were filled with cabs and buses, the sidewalks packed with jostling crowds of people all rushing to wherever it was that they worked. He watched them and felt nothing but contempt for the way in which they slavishly followed the routines that others forced upon them. At least he and his students would be able to pass unnoticed among this seething mass of commuters. Nero's face was unfortunately not completely unknown to the forces of law and order, so the less attention they drew to themselves, the better.

'How far is it?' Otto asked as he followed Nero on to the sidewalk.

'Just a few blocks,' Nero replied. 'You are both clear on your roles?'

Otto and Wing nodded. There had not been much time to refine the plan, so they had been forced to keep things simple, but sometimes that was the best way.

'If we're forced to improvise, then follow my lead as best you can,' Nero said quietly, scanning the crowd ahead for any sign of the police.

Otto tried to avoid looking like a tourist, but it was hard to resist the urge to goggle at the spectacle that surrounded them. In this part of town at this time of day it was like being stuck in a concrete canyon while an army and a circus passed each other in opposite directions. The sights, sounds and smells of the heart of the city were almost overwhelming, especially when he was used to the relatively calm surroundings of H.I.V.E. Otto frowned as a man pushed past him, bumping into his shoulder roughly without a word of apology. Nero had no such problems. Nobody seemed to jostle him or get in his way; he sailed through the ill-tempered crowd as if it wasn't even there.

As the three of them rounded the next corner they spotted the headquarters of Drake Industries. It was a towering edifice of mirrored glass with an intricate exo-skeleton of steel beams criss-crossing the surface. The building was set back from the street and in front of it was a wide plaza, the central feature of which was a huge sculpture of the Drake Industries logo. If corporations were the monarchs of the modern world, then this was definitely a fortress fit for a king. Nero, Otto and Wing joined the crowd of people who were pouring into the building, heading through the glass doors at the base of the tower and into the cavernous reception area. It bustled with activity as the workers around them made their way to the escalators and lifts. Security guards stood at choke points monitoring the employees as computerised systems scanned their ID cards. What wasn't so obvious were the sophisticated facial recognition systems that were tied into the array of cameras above each checkpoint, ensuring that the name on the badge matched the face of the person wearing it. Otto took all of this in with a glance as they walked towards the long, granite-topped reception desk, instantly memorising the positions of every single guard and camera that he could see and unconsciously building a three-dimensional map of their various fields of vision, hunting for blind spots and vulnerabilities. He could see very few flaws; security was as tight as one would expect for a company such as Drake Industries.

As they got closer to the desk, Otto let his senses extend outwards, brushing against the directory systems that fed into the receptionists' terminals. It took just a moment to find what he was looking for.

'Gina Charles, VP of Public Relations,' Otto said quietly to Nero, who gave an almost imperceptible nod in response.

The woman behind the reception desk smiled as they approached.

'Welcome to Drake Industries,' she said, still smiling. 'How can I help you today?'

'My name's Simon Jones,' Nero said, returning her smile. 'I'm here to see Gina Charles. She promised she'd give my son and his friend a tour of the building.'

'I see,' the receptionist said with a tiny frown. 'That's quite unusual. I'll have to speak to Mrs Charles about this.' She picked up the phone on her desk and punched in an extension number. After a few seconds she placed the phone back in its cradle.

'I'm afraid Mrs Charles is not in yet,' the receptionist said. 'If you'd like to take a seat, I'll let her know you're here just as soon as she arrives.' She gestured to an area filled with leather sofas off to one side of the reception area.

'Thanks, that's great,' Nero said and began to walk away. 'Oh, just one other thing,' he said stopping suddenly. 'Do you have a bathroom that my son could use? I'm afraid it was quite a long journey to get here this morning.'

'Of course,' the receptionist replied, 'it's just over there.'

She pointed to a door on the far side of the atrium.

Nero and Wing went and sat on the sofas while Otto headed into the visitors' bathroom. Shutting the door behind him, he quickly scanned the room, spotting what he needed in one of the cubicles. Unzipping his backpack and opening one of the concealed compartments inside, Otto pulled out a small vehicle with caterpillar tracks and a dark green canister mounted on top. He stepped up on to the toilet, balancing carefully as he levered open the ventilation hatch in the wall above his cubicle. The hatch was far too small for a person to climb through, but the compact tracked vehicle fitted inside with a couple of centimetres to spare. Otto resealed the hatch, climbed back down and flushed the toilet before unlocking the cubicle door and heading back out of the bathroom.

He went and sat down with Nero and Wing and reached into his backpack again, pulling out a small control unit with a screen in the middle and a tiny joystick off to one side. The screen lit up with the view from the tiny camera mounted on the front of the infiltration unit that he had just left in the bathroom ventilation shaft. He pushed forward on the joystick and inside the shaft the tiny vehicle began to move. To anyone watching in the reception area, Otto just looked like a teenage boy playing on his portable games console; they would never have guessed that what he was doing was anything but a game.

He steered the vehicle along the ventilation shaft for a couple of minutes before the camera showed that it had entered a larger chamber where several shafts connected. He panned the camera around the area and, once he was satisfied that it was in a suitable location, he pressed another button on the control unit and then switched it off, placing it back in his bag. In the depths of the ground-floor ventilation network a valve opened on the canister attached to the back of the tiny tracked vehicle and, with a hissing noise, it began to vent its contents.

Meanwhile, back in the reception area a confused-looking woman in an expensive suit approached Nero, Otto and Wing.

'Mr Jones,' the woman said with a frown as she walked up to them, 'I'm Gina Charles. Our receptionist has just explained to me that you're here to see me for a tour of the building. The only problem is we never let people tour the building and I don't have the slightest idea who you are. I'm afraid I'm going to have to ask you to –'

The woman was cut off in mid-sentence as the deafening ringing of fire bells filled the reception area. She looked shocked for a moment before hurrying back over to reception. The security guards dotted around the lobby rushed back towards the rear of the area, getting ready to direct the flood of people who were already starting to pour out of the stairwells. Smoke began to billow out of the vents in the ceiling, adding to the chaos as panic began to take over what was supposed to be a calm and orderly evacuation.

Nero watched the reception area fill up with smoke, waiting for the perfect moment. 'Now,' he said quietly, and all three of them got to their feet.

Otto walked quickly through the crowd of panicking employees, sticking to the route that he had already calculated would steer them through as many of the security system's blind spots as possible. Nero and Wing followed close behind. They had to bank on the fact that the building's automated security systems would never be able to cope with the number of people exiting the building and the thick grey smoke that was filling the area. They wove through the surging crowd to the nearest bank of lifts, all of which were now heading for the ground floor as part of the automated response to a fire alarm. Just as Nero, Otto and Wing reached the nearest lift, its doors slid apart and several worried-looking office workers hurried out.

'Onwards and upwards please, Mr Malpense,' Nero said calmly as the three of them stepped into the empty lift carriage. Otto closed his eyes and quickly connected with the simple systems that controlled the lifts. He effortlessly overrode the safety lockouts that were keeping their carriage on the ground floor and issued a new instruction for it to be sent to the executive level near the top of the building. The lift doors closed, muting the sounds of panic from the crowd that was now stampeding out of the building as the carriage began its ascent.

☻ ☻ ☻

Jason Drake stood looking through the glass that lined one side of his office. On the other side of the window was the vast underground hangar that contained the Dreadnought, which at that moment was alive with furious activity. He watched as robotic arms manoeuvred over the underside of the giant aircraft, making the modifications that they would need for the next stage of their plan. Everything was proceeding on schedule. Suddenly there was a knock at the door.

'Enter,' Drake said, turning away from the window as Furan walked into the room. 'What's wrong?' he asked, noting the other man's worried expression.

'There's something going on in New York,' Furan said quickly. 'There are reports of a fire at your headquarters building. An evacuation is under way.'

'Nero,' Drake said, his tone venomous. 'It has to be.'

'It seems unlikely to be merely coincidence,' Furan replied. 'I am having the security footage and Overwatch recordings analysed now, but I think there is little doubt that Nero has decided to bring the fight to us. He is not the sort of man to just run and hide.'

'Where is the retrieval team?' Drake asked quickly.

'They have arrived at Raven's presumed location. They are just about to launch their assault. Do you want me to divert them to the headquarters building?'

'No.' Drake rubbed his forehead with one hand. 'Have them despatch the hunter drones to stop Nero and inform building security there that we believe they have been infiltrated. I had hoped to take him alive, but he cannot be allowed to retrieve whatever it is he's looking for.' Drake feared that he knew exactly what Nero was after and there was no way he could allow him to discover the location of the hangar facility. 'The retrieval team will stay on Raven and can assist in Nero's capture or execution once we have his pet assassin in hand. Make sure your men understand that I want her alive. If Nero does slip through our fingers, I may need her as leverage.'

'As you wish,' Furan said and hurried out of the room.

Drake turned back to the window and tried to suppress the growing concern he felt. Nothing could be allowed to interfere with their plans at this point. He had to admit that he'd always felt a grudging respect for the man, even though he'd been so instrumental in Darkdoom's plan to take over G.L.O.V.E. He had even hoped that when they'd successfully carried out the next stage of their plan, Nero might see sense and ally with him and the rest of the

Disciples. It was too late for that now though. Nero had to be stopped at all costs and if that meant he had to die, then so be it.

☣ ☣ ☣

Raven tensed as a red light on the desk next to her terminal began to flash. That light meant something considerably bigger than a rat had just triggered the motion sensors in the sewer that served as this safe house's emergency exit. She quickly pulled up the feed from the camera that monitored the tunnel leading to the manhole cover at the rear of the basement. Moving stealthily along the tunnel towards the hatch were half a dozen heavily armed men in full body armour and gas masks. Raven swore under her breath and moved quickly to the rear of the basement, sliding four heavy bolts into place to lock the cover. She hurried back to her monitor and switched to the camera monitoring the street outside the safe house and was not surprised to see a similarly armed and equipped group climbing out of a large van parked directly outside. The team from H.I.V.E. were still several hours away and G.L.O.V.E. had no idea they were there, so whoever these men were they were certainly not there to protect her and the students.

'Everyone over here now,' Raven yelled at the surprised H.I.V.E. students.

'What's going on?' Nigel asked as they quickly moved over to where Raven was standing.

'Suffice to say that we're about to receive some uninvited guests,' Raven said, strapping her katanas to her back. 'Help me with this.' She gestured to the heavy metal table in the middle of the room. Shelby and Laura helped her tip the table over with a loud bang. 'Stay behind there,' Raven said, pointing at the overturned table. The students huddled behind it, taking advantage of what little cover it afforded.

Raven quickly moved to the switch on the wall and killed the lights, plunging the room into darkness. She heard a tiny sound as what she assumed was a breaching charge was attached to the front door. She took a deep breath, crouched down below the switch and pressed her hands hard over both her ears and closed her eyes. Moments later she heard the explosive bang of the breaching charge blowing the door's lock and then felt the concussive shocks from at least two flashbang stun grenades going off inside the room, their brilliant light still bright even through her tightly closed eyelids. She counted to three in her head and then in a single motion stood, flicked the light switch on and drew her twin swords.

The overhead lights flared brightly, immediately overloading the night-vision goggles of the three men who had entered the room. Taking advantage of their temporary blindness Raven rushed at them, her swords swinging. The crackling blades sliced through the two lead men's weapons effortlessly as she kicked the third man squarely in the centre of his mask, knocking him off his feet. Stepping past the two men with disabled guns, Raven dropped her swords and pulled a dangling stun grenade from each of their belts. She popped the pins from both grenades with her thumbs and threw them through the door into the middle of the remaining men who were about to enter the room. She kicked the door hard, forcing it shut just as the two grenades went off. There were yells from the men outside as the explosion instantly blinded and disorientated them.

The two men inside the room who remained conscious ripped their masks off, blinking in the bright light. Raven dropped low and punched the first man in the belly while sending her other foot out and hitting the second man's ankle with a sickening crunch. Raven gasped in pain as the shock ran up her injured leg; she staggered backwards clutching her thigh, inhaling sharply through her teeth. The man whose ankle she'd just broken collapsed to the floor with a yelp but the other man threw himself at her. The blow to his stomach had been absorbed by his body armour and now, having seen her pained reaction, he punched Raven hard in the wound in her thigh. Raven yelled out, collapsing to one knee as the blow sent waves of agony through her leg.

Shelby stood up from behind the table and moved quickly behind the man who was now drawing a vicious-looking combat knife from a sheath on his thigh and advancing on the crippled Raven. Shelby tapped the man on the shoulder and he spun around. She punched him squarely in the face and the man dropped the knife, stumbling backwards holding his shattered nose, blood pouring from under his hand. Shelby stepped towards him but was knocked to the ground by the enormous explosion that suddenly destroyed the bolted hatch at the rear of the room. Shelby and Raven fought to get to their feet as three more stun grenades flew into the room through the smoking mouth of the tunnel leading down to the sewers. The grenades rolled across the floor and then detonated with an ear-splitting bang just metres from Shelby and Raven.

Black-clad figures poured out of the hatch, fanning out across the room, levelling assault rifles. Raven tried to stand, half blinded and able to hear nothing but a high-pitched ringing sound. The lead man reached her and clubbed her back down with the butt of his gun. She fell unconscious to the ground next to Shelby. The other students, stunned and disorientated, slowly raised their hands in surrender as the soldiers from the sewers quickly surrounded them.

'This is retrieval team one,' the leader of the second assault team said into his throat microphone as he looked down at the battered figure that lay on the floor in front of him. 'Raven is secure; repeat, Raven is secure.'

☻ ☻ ☻

A nondescript black lorry was parked a couple of blocks from the safe house. Inside, several of Drake's men were sat at control consoles completing final checks on their systems. Their senior officer strolled down the centre of the large trailer, talking into his headset.

'Yes, sir, we have confirmation that Raven has been captured along with five of Nero's students. They are being taken to the nearest dropship for transport now.' He nodded, listening to the response on his headset. 'Understood. The hunter drones are ready for launch. They should be at the headquarters building within minutes. I shall despatch the uninjured members of the retrieval team to the location too. If Nero's there we'll find him.'

The man turned and addressed the men at the consoles.

'Launch all drones,' he said quickly. 'Use of lethal force has been authorised.'

The roof of a second lorry slid open and with a hushed whining sound three black shapes flew up out of the trailer and into the grey overcast sky.

The lift doors opened with a ding and Nero, Otto and Wing stepped out. This floor was one of several executive levels of the building and would normally have been bustling with activity at this time of day but was now silent and empty.

'We must move quickly,' Nero said. 'The smoke will already be starting to clear downstairs and it will probably not take the fire department long to realise that this was a false alarm.' As if in response to Nero's words, they could suddenly hear the distant wail of fire-truck sirens from the street far below.

'This layer of the company operates an isolated network,' Otto said as he closed his eyes. 'If I can get to a hub I should have almost unrestricted access.' Otto thought back to the schematics of the building that they had studied in the safe house earlier that morning. The layout of the offices on this floor meant there were only a couple of places that would be suitable to locate a wireless network hub. He could sense the buzzing flow of data around him and he tried to home in on which direction it was flowing from.

'This way,' Otto said after a few moments and hurried down the corridor with Nero and Wing close behind him. The humans may have left the building but the computers were still talking to one another. He followed the flow until they came to a door at the end of the corridor. Otto tried the handle. It was firmly locked and Otto realised with a vague sense of panic that it wasn't an electronic lock but a good old-fashioned mechanical one and consequently quite immune to his persuasion.

'Now would be a good time to have Shelby here,' Otto said with a frown. There wasn't a lock made that she couldn't master.

'Allow me,' Wing said and bent to examine it more closely. He stood back up slowly and then kicked the door just above the handle, smashing it open. The force of Wing's kick had almost knocked the door out of its frame; it now hung limply off just one hinge, the lock mechanism completely destroyed.

'Now that's what I call lock picking,' Otto said with a grin, pushing the shattered door aside.

'Perhaps not quite as elegant as Miss Trinity's work though,' Nero said with a slight smile.

Inside the room was a grey metal box from which a thick bundle of fibre-optic cable fed into the wall. All of the computers on this floor would communicate wirelessly with this hub, but the hub itself would communicate with the central mainframe through the cable since it was faster, more reliable and, theoretically at least, more secure. It was this connection that Otto needed: it was his route in.

He stepped forward placing his hands on the cool metal skin of the hub and closed his eyes. The flow of data through the system was like a fast-moving river and Otto allowed himself to be swept along by the current and carried to whatever destination it chose. He needed to get to the root of the network before he could begin to properly search for the information he needed and this was the quickest way to get there.

Nero watched as Otto stood completely immobile, the only sign of life was the slight movement of his closed eyelids, like a sleeper caught in a vivid dream. There was no doubt that he had a unique ability, but ever since he had discovered the truth of Otto's origins Nero had worried about where those gifts may one day lead the boy. The last thing he wanted was for Otto Malpense to follow in his 'father's' footsteps.

'We have company,' Wing said quietly from outside the hub-room door. Nero moved quickly to where Wing was watching the rest of the floor through the glass partitions that separated the various executives' offices. Several dark shapes could be seen moving along the corridor on the other side of the floor, directly between the three of them and the lifts. Nero glanced back at Otto, who was still standing like a statue with one hand on the hub. They needed to buy more time. He gestured for Wing to follow him and crept up the corridor towards the nearest junction. There were two concrete pillars here, one on either side of the junction, and as Nero pressed himself flat against one, Wing followed suit on the other side of the gap. Moments later they heard the sound of someone speaking quietly coming from the adjoining corridor.

'They gotta be here somewhere,' the voice said. 'The lift stopped on this floor.'

'Stay sharp,' another whispered voice replied. 'Just 'cos we ain't found 'em yet doesn't mean they ain't here.'

Nero glanced over at Wing, who gave a small nod. He tensed as the footsteps got nearer, waiting for the perfect moment. Just as the pistol in the outstretched hands of the first guard came into view, he struck, delivering an open-palmed chop to the man's wrist. The gun dropped from the startled man's now numb hand and he yelped in pain as Wing grabbed his wrist and pulled. Wing stepped past the guard as he staggered towards him and wrapped his bent arm around the man's neck. Wing pushed the back of the guard's head with his other hand, closing the choke hold and compressing the carotid arteries on each side of his neck, severing the flow of oxygenated blood to the man's brain. The second guard raised his pistol, trying to draw a bead on Wing, who was now standing behind the man's colleague, giving him no clear shot. He barely even registered Nero's presence behind him before a sharp blow to the base of his skull sent him collapsing to the ground. The man that Wing was holding struggled for a few moments before he too succumbed to unconscious-ness. The fight, if that was what it could be called, had lasted a matter of seconds.

Nero quickly pulled a pair of handcuffs from the guard's belt and snapped them closed on the unconscious man's wrists. Wing did the same to the other guard and they dragged the disabled men into one of the nearby offices.

'Good work,' Nero said as he closed the door. Wing had moved with the speed and skill that Nero would have expected from a student who had been personally tutored by Raven.

'They were poorly trained,' Wing said calmly. 'Let us hope the rest of the building's security team is too.'

Wing and Nero hurried back to the hub room. Nero knew it was only a matter of time now before somebody noticed that the security guards sent to check on this floor had not reported in. Otto had better find what they needed soon.

Inside the building's network, Otto searched desper-ately for any information that might give him a clue to the location of the Dreadnought's construction facility. Swarms of data surrounded him, covering everything from the blueprints of black-budget military research projects to the details of the stock levels in the vending machines throughout the building. The problem was that he was searching for something that wasn't actually there; he was looking for the hole in the records that the secret project had left. Suddenly something distracted Otto; once again he felt another presence there with him. He spun around searching for any sign of this phantom companion but could see nothing other than the whirling vortex of information that surrounded him on all sides.

'*Let me help you,*' a calm, reassuring voice whispered in his ear.

Otto felt a sudden surge of power. The apparently random threads of data that surrounded him seemed to coalesce into meaningful patterns. He could see their structure, sense their shapes and more than that he could see where pieces were missing: a deleted purchase order, an altered shipping manifest, payments to front companies, all of it pointing to one location. He had what he needed, he had to go, but something stopped him from disconnecting.

'Who are you?' Otto said to the empty space around him.

'A *friend*,' came the whispered response.

There was only one explanation that Otto could think of, something he had not dared to allow himself to believe.

'H.I.V.E.mind . . . is that you?' Otto said quietly. He waited for a reply but there was none and the unusual feeling of another presence being alongside him had vanished too.

Back in the hub room Nero frowned as he saw Otto's body tense and his eyes fly open. There was nothing behind the boy's eyes; he looked like he was staring at something invisible hanging in the air. Then with an explosive gasp Otto was back, blinking rapidly as he placed his other hand against the wall to steady himself.

'I've got it,' Otto said. 'Drake's facility is somewhere in Nevada. I can try to get a more precise location but it's going to take more time.'

'Time is the one thing we don't have,' Nero said. 'We have all that we're going to get today, gentlemen. I suggest we leave before we outstay our welcome.'

The three of them headed back down the corridor between the glass-walled offices, making for the stairs. Suddenly, Otto caught a glimpse of something moving out of the corner of his eye. A mechanical black shape rose up into the air outside the building and Otto just had time to make out the twin turbine pods on either side of the hovering machine before the object was obscured by a pair of bright muzzle flashes and the glass all around them exploded. Nero and Wing dived for cover as the heavy-machine-gun rounds tore through the side of the building and shattered the glass walls all around them in a blizzard of crystal shards. Office furniture was shredded and desktop monitors exploded as the bullets tore through the offices. Otto pressed himself against one of the concrete support pillars that were positioned regularly throughout the floor as the machine-gun fire suddenly stopped. Wing and Nero ducked and ran for the cover of another, larger support column further down the corridor. Suddenly the sounds of sirens and people shouting on the street far below were much clearer, but above those noises Otto could also hear the high-pitched whine of the machine's turbines as it manoeuvred around outside the building, looking for a better angle on its targets.

'Otto!' Wing yelled to get his friend's attention and pointed at something on the opposite side of the floor.

Otto looked in the direction Wing was pointing and saw another drone hovering in the air on the other side of the building, as if waiting for its partner to flush its targets that way. The columns they were hiding behind would not provide cover for long if they were attacked from both directions. Otto's mind raced. There was no way they could get to the stairs while those things were waiting for them, but every moment they stayed where they were brought the security teams that were doubtless converging on their position closer. They had to move and they had to move *now*. He closed his eyes and reached out with his abilities to see if he could exert any measure of control over the deadly machines, but they were either too far away or too well shielded against electromagnetic interference and he could sense nothing but the faintest shadow of their on-board systems, nowhere near enough for him to get a grip on and try to control them. They were going to have to do this the old-fashioned way. Otto pulled the pack off his back and unzipped it.

'Wing! I need you to get that thing's attention,' Otto shouted to his friend as he found what he'd been looking for. Wing nodded and sprinted from the column he had been taking cover behind towards the next column thirty metres or so further down the corridor. The drone's twin heavy machine guns roared into life once more, shattering more of the glass walls and tearing up the floor at Wing's heels. Wing reached the cover of the pillar but the drone did not stop firing; instead it just tore away at the column, blowing off huge chunks of the concrete, revealing the steel reinforcing rods inside.

Otto stepped out from behind his own column and fired the grappler unit that he now had strapped to his wrist. The bolt shot across the gap between Otto and the drone, trailing mono-filament wire. It struck the drone and pierced its metal outer casing, locking in place. Otto sprinted across the floor towards the shattered remains of the floor-to-ceiling glass that had once formed the outer skin of the building and without hesitation threw himself out into the void.

For a few sickening moments he fell, just able to hear the screams from the crowd that had gathered below above the noise of the wind rushing past his head. Then the line attaching him to the drone went taut and he swung out under the machine as it tipped crazily. The whine from the drone's turbines rose to a screech as the machine fought to stay airborne with this extra burden. Otto had no idea if the thing would be able to stay in the air with the addition of his weight but it was a chance he had had to take.

He hit the control to retract the grappler cable and raced upwards towards the stricken drone, grabbing at the metal framework that supported the guns beneath it as he released the grappler bolt. The drone spun, trying to shake him loose, but Otto clung on for dear life. He could see a pair of cameras mounted between the machine guns and realised that destroying them would blind the machine. He kicked at the cameras, smashing them with his foot as the drone pitched crazily. Otto tried not to think of the lethal drop beneath him as he fought to maintain his hold on the wildly bucking machine.

Suddenly he noticed a louder whine of turbines above the ailing engine noise of the drone he was hanging from. A second drone rounded the far corner of the building, trained its guns on Otto's dangling body and opened fire. Otto pulled himself upwards, hooking his feet around the body of the drone as the bullets ripped through the air where his waist had been just a moment before. The second drone drew closer, the guns tracking upwards, and Otto closed his eyes.

Nero opened fire through one of the building's shattered windows, a pistol from one of the downed security guards in each hand. The bullets hammered into the second drone's engine cowlings in a shower of sparks and flame as Nero kept firing. The drone tried to right itself, attempting to bring its own guns to bear on its attacker before it exploded in a black and orange ball of smoke and fire. Debris from the explosion smashed into the drone that Otto was hanging from and there was a terminal-sounding crunch as shrapnel was sucked into one of the machine's engines and it began to belch thick black smoke. The drone lurched sickeningly, almost breaking Otto's weakening grip as it spun out of control. Otto could hear the one remaining good engine screaming as it fought to compensate for the loss of its twin and he knew that he had just seconds. He pointed his arm towards the Drake building and fired the grappler, letting go of the drone almost simultaneously. The grappler bolt penetrated one of the steel beams that criss-crossed the outside of the building just above the shattered windows of the executive floor and Otto swung towards it, hitting the mirrored glass with a crunch as the drone he had been hanging from just a moment before spiralled out of control into the building across the street and exploded. Otto hit the control to reel in the cable and the grappler hauled him upwards towards the gaping hole that the machine guns had carved in the side of the building. As he reached the executive floor, Wing and Nero pulled him inside and gently lowered him to the ground.

'Can you walk?' Nero asked.

'Yeah, I think so,' Otto said, wincing as the flow of adrenalin slowed and his battered body began to let him know that it really didn't appreciate being treated like that.

'Good,' Nero said. 'We have to get moving now before the authorities completely seal off the area.'

'I owe you one,' Wing said quickly, placing a hand on Otto's shoulder. 'You saved my life.'

'Forget it,' Otto said with a grin. 'Besides, who's even keeping count any more.'

☢ ☢ ☢

Inside the black truck, several kilometres away, the commander of the hunter drone team paced back and forth along the length of the disguised control centre. He did not want to be the one who had to report to Jason Drake that the targets had escaped.

'They must still be inside the building,' reasoned one of

the men at the consoles that lined the narrow room. 'The police have it completely locked down.'

'I wouldn't be so sure about that. Has the retrieval team arrived on site yet?'

'Yes, sir, but they can't get through the perimeter that the police have set up. They can't help as long as the targets are inside the cordon.'

The commander stopped pacing for a moment and pinched the bridge of his nose. This operation was proving to be more difficult than he had hoped. He let out a long sigh and turned to one of his men.

'Launch the last two hunter drones,' he ordered, 'and have Overwatch scan the entire area surrounding the headquarters building for any sign of them. They haven't gotten away yet.'

chapter six

'I seem to recall saying that I wasn't going to do this,'
Nero said with a sigh, shining the torch ahead of them.
He, Otto and Wing trudged through the fetid sewer
leading away from the Drake Industries building. Otto had
overridden the lock that had been put on the tower's
elevator system and had got them down into the sub-
basement of the building. From there it had been relatively
easy to find a hatch leading into the sewers. The fact that
it had been easy did not, however, make it pleasant.

'So what were those things up there?' Otto asked Nero
as they walked slowly and carefully along the narrow
tunnel. You did not want to trip and fall over here.

'More of Drake's toys, I suspect,' Nero said angrily. 'He
has always been keen on using machines to do his dirty
work for him.'

'Surely it will arouse suspicion that his own hardware
attacked the building,' Wing said.

'I fear those drones were developed originally for G.L.O.V.E.'s use,' Nero replied. 'It's highly unlikely that anyone working for the security services will be able to connect them to Drake Industries in any way.'

They reached the end of the tunnel and walked out on to a metal gantry bolted to the wall surrounding a water-filled chamber.

'We appear to have run out of sewer,' Nero said with a sigh. The only way out was to climb up the ladder leading from the gantry to a manhole cover above. It was either that or go swimming in the murky brown water below, and they weren't quite that desperate yet.

'How far from the building are we?' Otto asked.

'Perhaps three hundred metres,' Wing replied, 'which, with luck, should be far enough to put us outside any police perimeter.'

'Very well,' Nero said, looking up at the thin beams of light coming through the tiny holes in the manhole cover, 'follow me.'

Nero climbed carefully up the rusty ladder with Otto and Wing close behind. As he reached the top he lifted the cover just a centimetre or so and peeked through the gap. After a few seconds Nero pushed the cover up further and slid it to one side. The three of them climbed out into a deserted alley between two tall office buildings. At the far end of the alley they could see the flashing red and blue lights of the emergency vehicles that now filled the plaza outside the Drake Industries building. At the other end of the alley sat a police car that was presumably maintaining the cordon that had been thrown up around the incident site. In front of the patrol car, two cops stood drinking coffee and watching the crowd of curious onlookers that had gathered.

'We'll have to head back towards the plaza,' Nero said with a frown. 'The police may not be specifically looking for us yet, but strolling out of a secure area right in front of them is not a chance we can afford to take.'

They started walking, checking the doors into the buildings on either side of them as they went, but they were all firmly locked. The only way out was the plaza end of the alley. As they got nearer they could see that there was a fire truck parked across the opening which would at least keep them hidden from view for the moment. Nero stopped, studying the big red emergency vehicle.

'I think I've got an idea,' he said with a slight smile. 'Wait here.'

He walked to the end of the alley and then to the front of the truck, signalling Otto and Wing to join him. They had to move fast before their narrow window of opportunity disappeared. Nero strolled calmly to the cab door of the fire truck, looked both ways to check they weren't being watched and pulled it open.

'Get in,' he instructed. Otto and Wing paused for a moment, unsure whether or not he was serious. The irritated frown that appeared on his face suggested that he was and they obediently climbed up into the cab.

'Pass me those,' Nero said, pointing to a spare fireman's coat and helmet that lay in the equipment area at the back of the cab. He took the uniform and quickly put it on, zipping the coat right up to his chin and pulling the helmet down low over his eyes, then climbed up into the truck. Nero looked around before ducking down under the dashboard and pulling a bundle of wires out from behind the steering column. He sorted through the brightly coloured wires until he found the two he needed and twisted together the exposed copper at their ends. A couple of seconds later the fire truck's massive engine rumbled into life.

'Stay down,' Nero said to Otto and Wing, steering the truck towards the gap in the secure cordon that a police officer was guarding. As the truck rumbled towards the exit the cop walked over to the driver's side and tapped on the window, which Nero dutifully wound down.

'You all done here?' the officer asked, looking confused.

'Nah, the chief wants me to head down the station and pick up a coupla spare oxygen tanks. We ain't got enough,' Nero said in a flawless New York accent.

'OK, see you later,' the cop replied and waved the truck

through the perimeter. Nero stepped on the gas and steered the truck carefully through the opening and turned on to the adjoining street. As he saw the police car vanish from sight in his rear-view mirror, he took off the helmet and put it on the seat next to him.

'Not bad,' Otto said, climbing up from the seat well where he'd been hiding.

'It's been a while since I've had to hot-wire a vehicle,' Nero said with a smile, 'but I suppose one just never forgets certain things. Such are the benefits of a misspent youth.'

Nero didn't notice the black van parked on the side of the road as they passed it but the driver of the van certainly noticed Nero. He started the engine and performed a U-turn into traffic, a few cars behind the fire truck. He picked up a radio handset and spoke quickly into it.

'Retrieval team to control,' the man said, 'I have a positive ID on Nero. He's heading west driving a New York Fire Department vehicle.'

'Repeat please, retrieval team,' a voice crackled back over the radio. 'Did you just say he was driving a fire truck?'

'Roger that, control,' the man said with a slight frown. 'I'm on his tail. Should I engage now?'

'Hold for drone support, retrieval team,' the voice on

the radio replied. 'Hunters are inbound to your location.'

☹ ☹ ☹

Shelby studied the bulky shackles securing her wrists as she walked slowly along behind Raven. These were unlike any she had seen before and the lack of a keyhole meant they were obviously locked and unlocked by some kind of remote device. There was no way that even Shelby was going to be able to get them off, not without all her tools anyway. Raven was limping quite badly and was clearly in some pain. The beating she had taken at the hands of the retrieval team had continued after she had regained consciousness. The H.I.V.E. students had watched on in horror as the soldiers had taken turns, paying particular attention to the bullet wound in her thigh. Horrific as her treatment had been, she had not given them the satisfaction of crying out in pain even once, something that Shelby could not help but admire. The six of them were herded into an abandoned train yard and lined up next to an old carriage. Two of the soldiers kept their weapons trained on Raven and the others while their squad leader walked far enough away not to be overheard as he talked into his radio.

'Anyone got any bright ideas about how we get out of this?' Laura whispered.

'Nero, Otto and Wing are still out there,' Nigel said

quietly. 'They'll find us. Don't worry.'

'Hey, kid, what part of total silence you having a hard part understanding?' the nearest soldier said aggressively, walking towards Nigel.

'I'm not afraid of you,' Nigel said firmly.

'Oh really?' the guard said. 'Let's see if we can't do something about that.' Without warning he hit Nigel hard in the stomach with the butt of his rifle and he collapsed to the ground, gasping for air.

'Leave him alone!' Franz yelled, taking a couple of steps towards the man.

'You want some too, fat boy?' the guard sneered and backhanded him hard across the face, dropping him to his knees next to Nigel.

'Hey! You piece of dirt,' Raven spat, 'why don't you pick on someone your own size?'

The guard walked over to her with a vicious grin on his face.

'What, you haven't had enough already?' The man laughed and kicked the wound in her thigh. Raven sank to one knee, breath hissing between her teeth.

'Anything else to say?' the guard said, leaning over her.

Raven powered upwards, the top of her head smashing into the middle of the guard's face. He didn't even make a noise, just collapsed backwards like a felled tree. Raven stepped forward and spat on the fallen man just as the other guard came running over and jammed a taser into her rib cage. She collapsed to the ground, convulsing as the guard reached down and shook his comrade. There was no response from the fallen man and he quickly pressed his fingers to the man's neck, feeling for a pulse. There was none. A look of fury appeared on the soldier's face and he stepped towards Raven, raising his rifle.

'Stop!' the squad leader yelled, striding towards them, his radio conversation finished. 'What do you think you're doing? Drake wants them all alive.'

'This witch just killed Karl,' the soldier spat, his rifle still levelled at the stunned Raven. 'She gets a bullet. I don't answer to Drake, only Furan, and he'd put her down like the rabid dog she is.'

'Fine,' the other man said, 'go ahead, as long as you don't mind explaining to Furan how you contravened a direct order. You know how well he responds to that.'

The other man said nothing for a few seconds and then lowered his rifle. All of Furan's men had seen or at least heard about what happened to those who disobeyed orders. It was, quite literally, a fate worse than death.

'Don't worry,' the squad leader said, 'she'll get what she deserves.'

There was a sudden rush of wind and a cloud of dust thirty metres away and a Shroud uncloaked, its rear loading ramp lowering to the ground. It looked more like a military aircraft than one of H.I.V.E.'s dropships, with a multi-barrelled cannon under its nose and twin missile pods on either side of the fuselage.

'You deal with Karl,' the commander said, 'I'll get the prisoners loaded.'

The soldier gestured with the barrel of his rifle for the H.I.V.E. students to get on board and they grudgingly complied. They had little choice, after all. Two more soldiers ran from the Shroud towards the squad leader.

'Take her on board,' the soldier ordered, pointing at Raven.

'What happened to Karl?' one of the men from the Shroud asked.

The squad leader nodded at Raven's unconscious body.

'She did.'

☹ ☹ ☹

'We seem to have acquired a tail,' Nero said as he turned the massive truck down another street. The black van that had been a permanent feature in the rear-view mirror for the past few minutes dutifully followed them on to the new road. The driver had always kept a couple of cars between himself and Nero's vehicle, but it was never further away than that. Nero made another unnecessary turn and yet again the van stuck with them.

'Who are they?' Otto asked.

'I don't know,' Nero replied. 'Not the police, that much is certain.'

'The truck may well have been reported stolen by now,' Wing said.

'True, but if it was the police they would have just pulled us over long ago. Whoever's in that van seems happy just to follow us for the moment.' Nero felt a growing sense of unease. If his gut was right and it was Drake's people behind them, he couldn't afford to lead them back to the safe house, but he still had to warn Raven that there were hostile operatives hunting them in the city. He pulled a slim silver phone from his inside pocket and punched in the number for the safe house. He let it ring for nearly a minute before hanging up.

'The safe house has been compromised,' Nero said, putting the phone back in his pocket with a frown.

'Are the others OK?' Otto asked, sounding worried.

'I'm afraid I don't know,' Nero said quickly, running through the scenarios in his head. Raven might have abandoned the safe house but he was sure she would have found some way of letting him know if that was what she had been forced to do. Given that she had five other H.I.V.E. students with her, she would only try to relocate them all if they were under direct threat. There was one other obvious option, of course, but Nero didn't want to think about that for the moment.

'Are you both strapped in?' Nero asked, studying the traffic on the road ahead. 'I'm almost ashamed to admit it but I've wanted to do this since I was five years old.' He flicked two big switches on the control panel mounted on the cab roof and the truck's sirens wailed into life and the red and white lights on the roof started to flash. Nero floored the accelerator as the cars on the road began dutifully to pull out of the way. Nero glanced in the rear-view mirror; the black van had pulled out from behind the cars that separated them and was roaring after them in pursuit.

'Look out!' Otto yelled as another drone, identical to the ones that had attacked them at the Drake Industries building, dropped out of the sky ahead of them and opened fire. Nero swerved as the machine-gun bullets tore into the body of the truck, just behind the cab. The truck side-swiped several cars that had pulled out of the way in front of them as it drunkenly rocked from side to side before coming back under control. The drone shot nimbly aside just moments before the truck would have ploughed into it and set off in pursuit of the speeding vehicle.

The black van was right behind them now and its driver swerved from side to side, trying to spot a gap in the traffic that would allow it to get ahead of the truck. Nero cursed under his breath as he saw the red lights ahead. Traffic was stationary leading up to the junction and cars were flowing across the road from the other direction.

Nero pulled over on to the wrong side of the road, spinning the steering wheel violently as he swerved to avoid the incoming traffic that was racing towards them with horns sounding and headlights flashing. The truck flew through the intersection at terrifying speed, clipping the rear of one of the city's distinctive bright yellow cabs and sending it spinning as the other traffic swerved in all directions, desperately trying to avoid further collisions.

The black van was still with them and was now drawing alongside the truck, the panel door in its side sliding open. Nero steered towards the van, trying to side-swipe it, but the driver reacted quickly and swerved away. At the same moment, a soldier in black body armour leapt from the doorway in the side of the van and caught hold of the short ladder that led up to the controls for the truck's main ladder. A moment later a second man made the same leap, his feet dragging along the road for a moment before he hauled himself up on to the back of the truck.

'We have unwanted passengers,' Nero yelled, as he jerked the wheel to one side to avoid a taxi that had pulled out in front of them.

'Leave them to me,' Wing said, unbuckling his lap belt. He opened the rear door and climbed carefully up on to the roof of the truck, trying to ignore the other vehicles that were whistling past just a couple of metres away. Nero kept the truck as steady as possible, but New York traffic was not designed for travelling at high speed in a vehicle that size. Wing looked back down the truck and saw the first of the two soldiers who had boarded the vehicle climbing up on to the main ladder that ran along its back. Wing too climbed up on to the ladder and began to crawl towards the middle of the truck. The soldier reached for the holster on his hip, drawing his pistol and aiming at Wing. He squeezed the trigger and the first round hit the metalwork of the ladder just in front of Wing with a metallic spang.

The hunter drone zipped past, heading for the truck's cab, quickly drawing level with it. Nero saw it at the last moment and swerved towards it just as the machine opened fire. Bullets tore through the cab as the drone ducked out of the way once again. Nero groaned and slumped sideways in the driver's seat.

Up on the ladder the sudden lurch caught the soldier who was aiming at Wing by surprise and he rolled off, flailing for a handhold, letting go of his pistol which bounced off the truck's bodywork and vanished over the side. Wing battled to hang on as the truck swerved wildly from side to side. Inside the cab Otto released his seatbelt and dived forward to grab the steering wheel as Nero collapsed on to the passenger seat. He fought to bring the truck under control, pushing his headmaster aside as gently as he could as he climbed into the driver's seat.

Otto jammed his foot back down on the accelerator and glanced over at Nero. There was a large gash on his forehead where a bullet had grazed his skull; he was out cold.

Wing scrambled along the ladder towards the soldier who was trying to climb back up on to it. Just as the man hauled himself up, Wing reached him and punched him squarely in the jaw. The man grunted and let go of the ladder, bouncing once on the truck's roof before rolling off and falling over the side. The black van swerved back behind the truck to avoid driving over the fallen man as his limp body hit the road. Wing saw the other soldier who had climbed on to the truck appear at the end of the ladder a couple of metres away, standing on the control platform. The man drew his pistol and began to raise it. Wing half ran, half dived along the last few metres of the ladder, grabbing one of the raised handholds on either side. He locked his arms and momentum did the rest, his body swinging forward, his legs kicking out and hitting the man square in the chest just as he fired his gun. Wing heard the bullet buzz past his head as the soldier sailed backwards off the truck, arms flailing wildly in the air. He hit the black van's windscreen and went straight through it, smashing into the driver and sending the vehicle veering wildly off to the right before it speared into a parked car at the side of the road, with an almighty crunch.

Otto saw a sign at the side of the road and he spun the steering wheel, sending the fire truck down a new street with a howling screech of protest from the tyres. Wing clung desperately on to the ladder control platform at the back of the truck as it tore around the corner, the wheels on one side almost leaving the ground. He heard a siren and two NYPD patrol cars shot out into the road behind them, the lights on their roofs flashing.

'Oh great,' Otto groaned as he spotted the police cars behind them. There was no way that the truck could outrun them. At that precise moment though, he had other things to worry about, as the hunter drone shot past Wing, along the length of the truck and out in front of the cab, the twin machine guns mounted beneath it swivelling around on their mounts to point backwards, directly at Otto. He dived beneath the dashboard as the drone opened fire, bullets tearing through the seat where his head had been just an instant before. The drone disappeared from view again as Otto popped back up. Ahead of them loomed the cavernous openings of the Queens Midtown tunnel, but the entrance for vehicles from this side of the East River was blocked by stationary traffic. He had to get into that tunnel – it might be the only way to shake off the drone before it killed them.

Otto took a deep breath as he steered the battered fire truck across to the other lane, straight into oncoming traffic. The vehicles speeding towards him did their best to get out of the way but within the narrow confines of the tunnel there was little room for manoeuvre. Otto cursed as the hunter drone appeared in his wing mirror again. He had hoped that the signal from whoever was controlling the deadly machine would not be able to penetrate the tunnel. Either they were not yet far enough inside or the systems controlling the drone were significantly more advanced than he had assumed.

Alongside, the drone drew level with the truck's right front wheel arch and opened fire. The machine-gun rounds ripped the speeding truck's heavy tyre to shreds in an instant and Otto felt the truck swerve violently, the steering wheel spinning wildly through his hands. He gasped as the truck tipped on to its side with a deafening bang and his world turned into a tumbling chaos of screeching metal and shattering glass. The stricken fire truck slid along the road in a shower of sparks before grinding to a shuddering halt. The other vehicles in the tunnel had nowhere to go. The wrecked truck blocked both lanes of the tunnel and drivers lost control as they tried vainly to stop their vehicles in time. First one car and then another slid sideways into the top of the truck with the sound of crunching metal.

It was a scene of chaos in the tunnel as Otto came to with a groan. At least one of the cars that had crashed into the truck had caught fire, its driver staggering away as the tunnel began to fill with dark smoke. Otto put his arms under Nero's armpits and, with a groan of exertion, began to drag the man's limp body out of the truck's shattered cab. He knew that he had to move quickly before the fire really caught hold, but his battered body was exhausted and Nero seemed impossibly heavy all of a sudden. He was halfway out of the cab with Nero when a horribly familiar black metallic shape appeared from over the top of the wrecked vehicle. The drone hovered in the air for a moment, scanning its surroundings, before drifting downwards, its guns rotating towards them. With an animal yell, Wing leapt from the top of the wreckage, swinging a bright red fire axe with every fibre of his strength. The axe hit the drone in one of its turbine pods, sending it spinning as Wing wrenched the axe free and swung it again, smashing into the middle of the drone's body and destroying the cameras and sensitive electronics that controlled it. The drone spun out of control, thrusting straight up into the tunnel ceiling before crashing back down again into the burning wreckage of the car that had hit the truck. Wing collapsed to his knees, and let the axe fall from his hands. He had a vicious graze that covered one side of his torso and he was bleeding from multiple lacerations.

'You look like someone threw you from a moving

vehicle,' Otto said with a pained smile.

'Not an experience I'm in a hurry to repeat,' he replied. 'Is he alive?' He asked, pointing at Nero.

'Yeah,' Otto said. 'Can you help me carry him? We've got to get out of here.'

Wing nodded and slowly got to his feet. He and Otto lifted Nero up between them and slowly walked away from the wreckage, joining the hundreds of people making their way out of the tunnel and towards daylight.

☢ ☢ ☢

The Shroud carrying Raven and the other prisoners touched down on the landing pad as the huge sliding doors overhead closed, sealing them below the desert floor. Pietor Furan watched as a dozen men surrounded the tail of the Shroud, weapons ready. He knew from personal experience that it was unwise to take any chances with one particular prisoner on board this aircraft. The loading ramp dropped down and after a few seconds Raven limped out on to the landing pad. She had a gash on her forehead and her face was half covered in dried blood, but there was still a look of defiance on her face.

'Privet Natalya,' Furan said, greeting her in Russian as she approached, 'it is good to see you again.'

Raven's eyes widened as she saw him and she froze,

standing motionless as he walked towards her. Somewhere inside her head a voice that she had not heard for years was screaming at her to run, to hide. She ignored it as best she could.

'I should have known that scum like you would be involved with this,' Raven spat on the ground at his feet, 'you treacherous piece of filth.'

'Come now, Natalya,' Furan said with a vicious smile, 'is that any way to greet an old friend?'

'Take these off,' Raven said, holding her shackled wrists up in front of her, 'and I'll greet you properly.' She had murder in her eyes.

'Ah, you never change, Natalya – that's one of the things I've always liked about you,' Furan said, smiling. 'And I see you even brought some of your young charges along.'

Behind Raven, Franz and Nigel walked slowly down the ramp, glancing at the soldiers around them nervously. Just behind them were Shelby, Laura and Lucy, taking in their new surroundings with expressions of exhausted resignation.

'You know, I never understood why you wanted to help Nero with his efforts to turn G.L.O.V.E.'s brats into useful operatives. The great leaders of our world are not manufactured like this.' He gestured at the group of students. 'They are born in blood, in the war zone or on the streets, like we were. Not in the classroom like battery chickens. Nero has always been an idealistic fool, but I would have expected better from you, Natalya.'

'He's a better man than you will ever be,' Raven growled. 'At least he understands the concepts of loyalty and honour.'

'Honour?' Furan laughed. 'There's no place for honour in our world. You sound just like that spineless fool Darkdoom. G.L.O.V.E. was never about honour; it was about power, control, ruthlessness – at least it used to be. But G.L.O.V.E. lost its way when Number One died and now it must be swept aside and replaced by a new order, a group that understands; that we rule through strength and fear, not misguided principles of honour. In time you will understand; in time you will join us.'

'I would die before helping you,' Raven snarled.

'Nyet, Natalya,' Furan said with an evil smile, taking her chin in his hand. 'I've broken you before and I'll break you again.' He let her go and gestured to the soldiers surrounding them. 'Take them away. Use maximum-security holding cells for all of them.'

☻ ☻ ☻

Nero groaned and his eyes flickered open.

'How are you feeling?' Otto asked.

Nero sat leaning against a wooden crate in a dingy

room. Shafts of light poured in through a cracked and dirty old skylight overhead, catching the dust that hung in the air. Wing stood nearby looking out through a crack in the planks of a boarded-up window.

'Other than the mother of all headaches, fine,' Nero said, gingerly touching the crease the drone's bullet had left in his forehead. 'Where are we?'

'In a warehouse on the east side of the river,' Otto replied. 'There was no way we could make it back to the safe house until you were on your feet again. Besides which, I wasn't sure it could strictly be called *safe* any more.'

'You did the right thing,' Nero said, standing up slowly. 'How long was I out?'

'A couple of hours,' Otto replied. 'I was just starting to get worried.'

'Oh, I've survived considerably worse than this before now, Mr Malpense,' Nero said with a pained smile. 'We need to work out our next move. Now we know the location of Drake's facility we need to prepare to mount an assault as soon as possible.'

'Shhhh!' Wing hissed from across the room, signalling that he could hear something outside.

Otto strained to hear what it was that caught his friend's attention and after a couple of seconds he could just pick up the sound of boots on concrete, and they were getting closer. Nero, Otto and Wing moved away from the door, backing into the shadows at the rear of the room as the sounds of running footsteps got louder and louder. Suddenly the sound stopped, and a moment later the door to the room was kicked in with a crash, half a dozen men in black body armour and face masks fanning out into the room, weapons raised. Wing stepped out of the shadows, assuming a defensive stance, determined at least to go down fighting.

The lead soldier lowered his weapon and pulled off his mask.

'There'll be no need for that, Mr Fanchu,' Colonel Francisco said with a slight smile. 'If we're going to stop Jason Drake I'm going to need all my men in one piece, if you don't mind.'

chapter seven

'Thank you for getting here so quickly, Colonel,' Nero said as they walked to where Francisco's squad had assembled in the warehouse.

'Once we got within range and were able to lock on to the transponder in your Blackbox it didn't take us long to track you down but judging by the news reports I've been following on the way here you could have done with our help a couple of hours ago,' Francisco replied, raising an eyebrow.

'It has been rather an eventful day, yes,' Nero said, smiling weakly. 'It would have been a lot worse if it had not been for those two though.' He nodded towards Otto and Wing, who were sat nearby being checked out and patched up by the squad's field medic.

Suddenly, one of Francisco's men came running into the warehouse.

'Sir,' the man said as he approached Nero and the

Colonel, 'we've just received a report from team two. The safe house that Doctor Nero directed us to has been attacked. It looks like they were hit hard and fast. There's no sign of Raven or the students.'

'Damn it,' Nero hissed. He had felt in his gut that something had gone badly wrong but he'd hoped that somehow Natalya would have been able to escape. It was clear now that was not the case. 'How did Drake find us?'

'I think I may have the answer to that,' Professor Pike said, walking towards them.

'It's unusual to see you away from the school, Professor,' Nero said as the old man approached.

'I was led to believe that it was an emergency,' the Professor said with a smile. 'Drop everything, highest priority, all hands on deck, that sort of thing. Besides which, I had some new equipment that I thought might come in useful and there was no way I was letting the Colonel and his men use it until they'd been fully briefed.'

'Yes, the Professor spent much of the journey here briefing us,' the Colonel said, rolling his eyes. 'It was a *very* long journey.'

'You have something for us, Professor?' Nero said, gesturing at the papers that Pike was holding.

'Yes, I suspect this is how Mr Drake has been tracking you,' the Professor said, handing Nero one of the sheets. It was a blueprint of what looked like a satellite. 'Project

Overwatch, a military black-budget contract that Drake Industries was working on. I have some old friends in the R&D department at the Pentagon and they were kind enough to furnish me with these drawings. Judging by its specification, it is designed to render the concept of a ground-based manhunt quite redundant. If you can see the sky, then you can be identified and tracked. Quite impressive actually. The physical-profile reconstruction algorithms must be very advanced. I'd love to have a look at them.'

'Was there anything else that your friend was able to tell you?' Nero asked, handing the schematic back to the Professor.

'Apparently it was launched with another satellite that Drake Industries did not work on – a deep black military project that even my friend could find out nothing about, other than the name of the project: Thor's Hammer. The two were designed to work in unison somehow, but beyond that he could tell me nothing.'

'Thank you, Professor,' Nero said, 'that is most helpful. Drake must have tracked me back to the safe house earlier today and hit it soon after we left. Could he have tracked us here?'

'It's possible,' the Professor replied, 'so I suggest that we relocate sooner rather than later.'

'Agreed,' Nero said. 'Colonel, get everyone on to the

Shrouds. I'll brief you on the next mission once we're airborne.'

☣ ☣ ☣

'That is most disappointing,' the figure on the screen in front of Drake said.

'We will reacquire Nero,' Drake replied, sounding more confident than he felt.

'He cannot be allowed to interfere. We've spent too long planning this for our efforts to be derailed by a glorified school teacher,' the figure on the left-hand screen said.

The faces of the people on the three screens were all digitally disguised, their features distorting and blurring in such a way that while one might be able to determine their race or sex, that was about as much as could be distinguished. To Drake they were known simply as the Disciples and that was all he needed to know.

'It's unfortunate that Nero became involved,' the figure on the right-hand screen said, 'but we have Raven and five of his students. That gives us leverage. Nero will not sacrifice them lightly.'

'Does he know about the Nevada facility?' the woman on the left asked.

'I'm not sure,' Drake replied calmly. 'A network intrusion was recorded while Nero and two of his students were inside the headquarters building in New York, but it was only brief, and the system contains no records of this location. I don't believe they could have discovered our whereabouts.'

'Nero was accompanied by his students?' the man on the centre screen asked quickly.

'Yes, two boys were with him,' Drake said, pulling up the blurry security camera images of Nero and his companions that had been forwarded to him.

'There, the boy with the white hair,' the man on the right said with quiet venom. 'Malpense.'

'Should I know who that is?' Drake asked.

'No, his involvement in the death of Number One was kept from the ruling council,' the woman said. 'Nero has always done whatever he could to keep Mr Malpense out of the limelight, but he was there when Number One was killed, we know that much. We also know that if he got access to your files then the location of that facility is no longer a secret. Suffice to say, Otto Malpense has certain *unique* abilities.'

Drake studied the blurry image of the boy with the spiky white hair. He certainly didn't look particularly exceptional.

'It's too late for anyone to stop us now,' Drake said calmly. 'We're ready to proceed. Just a couple more hours and we'll be ready for launch. Everything is going precisely to schedule.'

'Good,' the man on the centre screen replied. 'The target will be at the coordinates we supplied. Make sure that everything is ready. It might be weeks before we get another opportunity.'

'Understood,' Drake replied and the screens in front of him went dark. He couldn't help but feel a genuine sense of excitement. In just a few hours' time the Disciples would remind the world what true villainy was and G.L.O.V.E. would effectively be destroyed in the process. A new day was about to dawn.

☻ ☻ ☻

'Nevada,' Colonel Francisco said, sounding a bit impatient.

'Yes,' Otto replied, studying the map that was laid out on top of the equipment trunk.

'And that's all you have?' the Colonel asked. 'You are, I assume, aware that it is quite a large state.'

'Two hundred and eighty-six thousand three hundred and sixty-seven square kilometres,' Otto said, unconsciously calculating the precise figure from the map in front of him.

'I think the Colonel wants to know if you can be any more specific,' Nero said with a slight smile.

Otto continued to stare at the map, the rumble of the Shroud's engines and the low murmur of conversation

154

from the troops on board seeming to fade away as he concentrated. They had been airborne for just a few minutes and they needed to give the pilot a precise destination.

'It has to be somewhere remote,' Otto said, sounding distracted, 'but somewhere that isn't going to attract people who want to enjoy the great outdoors. You don't want hikers stumbling into your secret launch facility.' He looked up at Nero. 'If you were going to build a facility here, where would you build it?'

Nero studied the map for a couple of minutes.

'There is one obvious location,' Nero replied. 'Remote, largely unpatrolled within its own perimeter, it looks ideal.' He pointed to a label on the map. It read 'Nuclear Test Site'.

'Well, I can see why you wouldn't have to worry about people wandering around,' Otto replied, 'but wouldn't that be too hostile an environment?'

'Parts of it, yes, but it's a huge area and there hasn't been a live nuclear test there in years,' Nero said quickly. 'It seems unlikely, I know, but that's precisely why I would build there. We know that Drake Industries has worked on black projects for the US military, so they may well have had access to the area for testing purposes. All of which would give Drake plenty of opportunity to scout for a suitable location under the cover of carrying out his legitimate business.'

'It's also somewhere where the locals are used to strange lights in the sky and mysterious aircraft. Look who's right next door.' Otto tapped his finger on a location on the map.

'Groom Lake,' the Colonel said.

'Or to give it its more common name, Area 51,' Otto said quickly. 'The perfect cover for experimental flights of any type of aircraft.'

'Also one of the most highly secured pieces of airspace in the world,' the Colonel said with a frown. 'Not a good place to be if you want to avoid detection by the military.'

'The Dreadnought can render itself invisible to the air force's technology,' Otto replied, 'at least for a short time. So that wouldn't be a problem. The benefits would outweigh the risks.'

'Even if you're right and this is where Drake's holed up, it's still a huge area. How are we going to find him? It's not like the air force are going to let us wander into a nuclear-weapon test site to have a quick look around.'

'We may not need to,' the Professor said, looking up from the stolen Overwatch schematics.

'You have an idea?' Nero asked.

'Perhaps,' the Professor said. 'What's the single most important raw material for a facility of this kind?'

'Power,' Nero replied after a moment. 'H.I.V.E. was

built on an island with an active volcano. Without that there would have been no geothermal power plant and without power there would have been no school.'

'Exactly,' the Professor said with a broad smile, 'and that's the one thing that Drake's facility will not be able to survive without.'

'Well, he can't be tapped into the national electrical grid,' Otto said quickly. 'That level of power consumption would be too obvious, too easy to trace.'

'So he must have an on-site power supply,' the Professor replied, 'something compact but extremely powerful. Possibly nuclear. The radiation in the environment would mask any environmental contamination.'

'No,' Otto said quietly, thinking back to the earlier events on the Dreadnought, 'a fusion core.'

'Yes, that would be ideal,' the Professor said, 'but it's just theoretical at this point. No one has been able to produce a working prototype.'

'Drake has,' Nero said quickly. 'The Dreadnought has one as its main power source. And if he installed one in the Dreadnought then it's reasonable to assume that he could also be using one to power the facility where it was built.'

'Fascinating,' the Professor said quietly. 'If Drake really has got a fusion generator working . . . I would love to see it.'

'The question at this point is not how it works,' Otto said, looking again at the map, 'but can we detect it?'

'I believe we could,' the Professor said, nodding. 'There are several satellites that might give us some clues. I need a few minutes.' He walked over to where his laptop rested on top of some equipment crates and began to type.

'I'm going to check on Wing,' Otto said as the Professor worked.

'Very well,' Nero replied. 'The Colonel and I need to discuss our tactical options.'

Otto walked away, leaving Nero and Francisco in hushed conversation. Wing sat at the far end of the Shroud's passenger compartment, naked from the waist up, his head resting against the bulkhead, wincing occasionally as a medic prodded at his injured ribs.

'So what's the verdict?' Otto said as he approached. 'Are you going to live?'

'It would appear so,' Wing said. He inhaled sharply through his teeth as the medic found yet another painful spot on the side of his chest.

'The abrasions are bad and they're going to hurt like hell for a while but they should heal up just fine,' the man said, reaching into his pack and pulling out a paper-wrapped gauze bandage. 'You've probably got a couple of cracked ribs; I can't tell for sure until we get you back to H.I.V.E. and perform some X-rays. I'll strap them up in the meantime but you still need to take it easy, give them a chance to heal. If you think you feel bad now, you really don't want to know what a punctured lung feels like, trust me.'

The medic began to wrap the bandage around Wing's chest, which Wing did not seem to be enjoying particularly. After a couple of minutes he was finished and he turned to Otto.

'Right, your turn. Sit down,' the medic instructed.

'I'm fine, really,' Otto said, holding his hands up in front of him.

'I'll be the judge of that,' the medic said, pointing at the seat next to Wing. 'Sit.'

Otto sighed and sat down as the medic pulled out a pen light and shone it into his eyes.

'Have they found Drake yet?' Wing said, carefully zipping up the black jumpsuit that he had been given to replace his shredded clothes.

'They're working on it,' Otto said. 'I just wish I could have got a more precise location. If I'd only had a few more minutes in the network.'

'You did all that you could,' Wing said, closing his eyes. 'There was no more time.'

'Tell that to Raven and the others,' Otto said unhappily. 'God alone knows what's happening to them right now.'

'They will survive. I have faith in their abilities. We will rescue them and stop Drake. That is what we do, remember?'

'You make it sound so simple,' Otto said as the medic pushed a scope inside his ear and stared into it.

'That is because it is simple,' Wing replied with a slight smile. 'The hard part will be listening to Shelby explain how she didn't need our help and that she was quite capable of escaping on her own, thank you very much.'

'I suppose you're right.' Otto chuckled.

'You're fine,' the medic said. 'Cuts and bruises, nothing life-threatening.' He closed his pack with a nod to Otto and Wing and walked away.

'I'm just going to go and see what the Professor's up to,' Otto said. 'You all right here?'

Wing didn't reply; he was too busy snoring.

'I wish I knew how you did that,' Otto said, standing up and shaking his head in disbelief. He walked over to where the Professor was busily typing away at his laptop.

'That should do,' the Professor said to himself as Otto approached.

'Progress?' Otto asked.

'Well, I believe I may have located a satellite that will serve our purposes,' the Professor replied, 'but it will take some time to access its control systems. I don't suppose you'd like to try your hand at accessing them, would you?'

'It's too far away,' Otto lied. The truth was he still couldn't shake that vague feeling of unease that accompanied the use of his abilities, and at the moment the last thing he wanted to do was push them to their limits. 'You really need Laura for something like this.'

'Yes, Miss Brand's skills would be most helpful,' the Professor said, flexing his fingers over the keyboard, 'but this old dog knows a few new tricks of his own.'

He continued to type and Otto watched for a few seconds until he could no longer follow what the Professor was doing. It reminded him of watching Laura, her fingers flying over the keyboard, unconsciously sticking the tip of her tongue out between her lips as she concentrated. Otto might be able to access computer systems but he did it by metaphorically kicking the door in: it was an unsubtle brute-force approach. He actually quite envied the elegant way that Laura, on the other hand, would just pick the lock, get in and then get out without anyone ever knowing she'd been there. He just hoped that he would get to see her do it again.

☻ ☻ ☻

'OK, this sucks,' Shelby said, kicking the heavy steel door of the cell that she was sharing with Laura and Lucy. The guards had found the lock-picking kit that she kept concealed in the sole of her shoe, but even if they hadn't there was no access to the locking mechanism from this side of the door. She was a thief, not a magician.

'Will you sit down and let me have a look at your head?' Laura asked, gesturing over to one of the three mattresses on top of concrete blocks that served as beds.

'I told you I'm fine,' Shelby snapped.

'Will you just let me have a look anyway?' Laura asked calmly.

'OK, OK. If it'll get you off my back,' Shelby said, sitting down on one of the beds with a sigh.

Laura ignored Shelby's bad mood. They were all scared of what might happen to them and Shelby in particular did not take kindly to being locked up. Laura supposed it must have been something to do with her old job. Shelby had, for a short time before becoming a student at H.I.V.E., been the Wraith, the world's most notorious jewel thief, and she had never been caught. As a consequence, being locked up like this was probably her worst fear and the effect it had on her mood was not pleasant. Laura carefully pushed aside her friend's blonde hair and inspected the nasty gash in her scalp that she had received back in the safe house.

'So, can you see my brain?' Shelby asked.

'Nope, but that's not really surprising. I don't have a microscope with me,' Laura replied.

'You see how I'm not laughing,' Shelby said.

162

'You'll be fine,' Laura said with a sigh. 'The cut could do with dressing but, to be honest, I think the last thing we need to worry about right now is an infected wound.'

'What do you think they're going to do with us?' Lucy asked, sitting down on the bed opposite.

'I'm actually trying not to think about it at the moment,' Shelby said. 'But I'm guessing it won't be a spa session and a sauna.'

'Do you think the others got away?' Lucy asked. 'Doctor Nero, Wing, Otto . . .'

'Oh, I wouldn't worry about those three,' Laura said quickly. 'When you've known them for as long as we have you'll realise that they're quite capable of looking after themselves.'

'I hope so,' Lucy replied. 'Wing's kind of quiet but you can tell he'd do anything for you. Otto's . . . well, Otto's just been really friendly and helpful since I arrived.'

'Hey, Brand, I think Otto may have another admirer,' Shelby said with a slight smile, glancing for the briefest of moments at Laura.

'Another?' Lucy asked.

'Oh, Otto's all right,' Laura said, her cheeks flushing, 'if you like the geeky type. Which I don't, incidentally.'

'This coming from someone whose desktop image on her computer at H.I.V.E. says "Han Shot First!"' Shelby said with a snort of laughter.

'I just hope we get to see them again,' Lucy said, looking over at the cell door. 'Actually, to be honest, it'd be enough if we get to see *anyone* again.'

☺ ☺ ☺

Darkdoom raised his head and looked up at Drake.

'Go to hell,' he spat, his voice ragged.

'Again,' Drake said, gesturing to the man at the nearby controls.

Darkdoom jerked upright, all the muscles in his body contracting in agony as electricity coursed through his body. The excruciating pain seemed to last for long minutes but it could only have really been a few seconds. As the current was cut, Darkdoom slumped backwards into the metal chair he was shackled to.

'Come now, Diabolus,' Drake said in a soothing tone, 'it doesn't have to be like this. Just read the text on the screen below the camera and this can all be over.'

'There's no way I'm going to read that,' Darkdoom whispered, his voice hoarse. 'I don't know what kind of nightmare you have planned, Drake, but you're not pinning it on G.L.O.V.E.'

'Oh, but I am,' Drake said, 'and you're going to help e.'

'I'll die first,' Darkdoom said, a look of grim determina- on his face.

'You know, I do believe you would,' Drake said with a sigh. 'I was hoping I wouldn't have to resort to this, but you leave me little choice.' He walked over to the cell door and knocked once. A moment later the door opened and the guard outside pushed Nigel into the room.

'Oh God . . . Nigel . . . are you OK?' Darkdoom said, feeling panic claw at his guts.

'He's fine,' Drake interrupted before Nigel could reply, 'at least for now. Now read the statement and there'll be no need for any unpleasantness.'

Darkdoom stared at Nigel. He could see the fear in his son's eyes but he also saw the tiny, almost imperceptible, shake of the head that was meant just for him.

'No,' Darkdoom said, looking down at the floor, 'not until you let him go.'

'I think you misunderstand the exact nature of your negotiating position,' Drake said, pulling a large black handgun from the shoulder holster concealed beneath his jacket. He pressed the pistol to Nigel's temple and cocked the hammer. 'Now, you'll start reading the statement into the camera by the time I count to three or I'll blow Junior's brains out all over the wall. I do hope I'm making myself perfectly clear.'

Darkdoom stared back at Drake. He had spent his life around people like him; some were honourable, some were psychotic and some were just plain evil, but one thing he had learnt from them all was how to spot when someone was bluffing. Drake was not.

'One . . . two . . .'

'Stop,' Darkdoom said, feeling an aching sense of despair. 'I'll do it, damn you.'

Drake gestured towards the camera, the pistol still pressed against Nigel's forehead. Darkdoom took a deep breath and stared straight at the lens.

'My name is Diabolus Darkdoom and I am the supreme commander of G.L.O.V.E., the Global League of Villainous Enterprises. I speak to you now to inform you that the events of today are just the beginning . . .'

chapter eight

'I'm in!' the Professor said triumphantly, rubbing his hands together. Flashing on the display of the laptop in front of him were the words 'Access Granted'.

'Good,' Nero said, walking over and looking at the screen. 'Will we be able to detect the energy signature of the fusion core?'

'Let's see, shall we?' the Professor said as Otto joined them. 'It's supposed to be just a geological-survey satellite, but its control interface was far too well protected. And here's why.' He pointed at something on the screen. 'It's not unusual for the military to piggyback their own sensors on to civilian satellites, but it's usually kept very quiet. Here they've bolted their own electromagnetic energy sensor on to the Geosat. Heaven only knows what they use it for, but it should be sensitive enough for us to detect the fusion core.'

The Professor typed a series of commands on the

keyboard and a high-resolution image of the area of Nevada surrounding the nuclear-testing site appeared on the screen. He punched in another command and the map was replaced by a dark blue map covered in white blotches of varying intensity.

'What we're looking at is the energy signature of the numerous nuclear detonations that have occurred in the area from the very first test in 1951 right through to the end of testing in the early nineties. There were over nine hundred detonations both above and below ground during that period, which will make detection of the core's specific signature difficult. Not so much a needle in a haystack as a piece of hay in a needlestack.'

'Another reason why Drake may have favoured the location in the first place,' Nero said.

'Indeed,' the Professor replied, 'but there are certain key differences that should help us. The biggest clue is that the core is still active and so it will have a constant energy reading. The residue from past explosions will have a decreasing reading, only a microscopic decrease over the time we have, but I'm hoping the sensors on board the satellite are sensitive enough to detect it.'

The Professor typed in another command. The display changed: now there were only two bright white spots on the map, both of them practically on top of each other.

'Two active fusion cores,' the Professor said with a smile.

'I believe we have a winner.'

'One for the facility and one on the Dreadnought, ' Otto said. 'That has to be it.'

'Colonel, prep your men,' Nero said. 'We have a target.'

⊛⊛⊛

'It's been a long time,' Furan said, circling Raven carefully, both hands raised in loose fists in front of him. He wore dark grey combat trousers and a white vest. He was in his fifties but he had a physique that was the product of years in the Spetsnaz, Russia's elite special forces unit, and then as a freelance assassin. What wasn't muscle was scar tissue.

'Not long enough,' Raven said angrily and aimed a high kick at his head. Furan side-stepped and blocked her kick with crossed arms. Raven struggled to keep her balance on her injured leg and half fell to the ground.

'You're slow, Natalya,' Furan said with a predatory grin. 'I know you're injured but still . . .'

He stepped towards her and aimed a punch at her stomach. Raven rolled with the blow but even though she had avoided most of the impact it was still enough to knock the wind out of her. She staggered backwards away from him.

'I thought I taught you better than that, girl,' Furan growled. 'Never retreat. Attack is always the best form of defence.'

Raven looked around; the room was empty, with just bare concrete walls. There were no environmental weapons that she could take advantage of. 'All you taught me was how it felt to be betrayed,' she said quietly.

'Betrayal? Hah! You failed me, Natalya. Everything that happened after that was just the inevitable consequence of that failure.'

'The only way I failed was in not killing you a long time ago,' Raven said through gritted teeth.

'You might have had a chance once, girl,' Furan replied, advancing on Raven again, 'but your new life has left you soft. Look what you've become.' He threw a lightning-fast jab at her face, which Raven just managed to block, but she could do nothing to stop the arcing blow to her ribs from his other fist. The impact nearly lifted her off her feet and she staggered backwards again.

'You're lazy . . .' He kicked at her wounded thigh and her leg collapsed under her. 'Slow . . .' He swung a vicious arcing kick into the other side of her ribs.

'And weak.'

He delivered a final savage punch to Raven's chin and she collapsed backwards, her breathing laboured, the whole room spinning around her. Furan stood over her with a look of triumph on his face.

'It's your choice, Natalya,' he said quietly. 'Join us or die along with Nero, Darkdoom and the rest of their pathetic organisation.'

'Go to hell,' Raven said, spitting blood on to the grey concrete floor.

'A shame. I had hoped we could be friends.' Furan went over to the steel door in the wall. He knocked twice and a guard opened the door to let him out. He turned and looked back at Raven, who was struggling to her feet, a look of defiance on her face.

'Such a waste of potential,' he said and walked out of the room. The steel door swung shut with a clang and heavy bolts slid into place. Raven leant against the wall beside her; she closed her eyes and tried hard to block out the pain, but she knew she couldn't take much more. Bad enough that she should have allowed herself to be captured, but now finding herself back in the hands of the one man in the world she truly feared was infinitely worse. She put her back against the wall and slowly slid down it until she was sitting on the floor.

'Where are you, Max?' she whispered to herself.

☢ ☢ ☢

'There's nothing there,' Francisco said, studying the photographs that the hijacked satellite had taken of the area that was supposed to contain Drake's base. 'Or that's what I'm meant to think anyway.'

'Exactly,' Nero said. 'Drake's gone underground . . .

literally.' Nero couldn't help but feel a tiny bit of respect for Drake. He knew how hard it was to construct these facilities and that was with the full support of G.L.O.V.E. and their specialists. To have built an underground hangar capable of taking the Dreadnought without any external assistance and while still keeping it secret was impressive, to say the least.

'My men will be sitting ducks out in the open like that,' the Colonel said, still studying the images. 'God only knows what sort of defensive systems Drake has installed. We can't put anyone on the ground until we've scouted a way in.'

'I think I know who could handle that,' Nero said quickly. He turned to where Professor Pike was unpacking various pieces of equipment from an armoured crate. 'Professor, did you bring the dropsuits?'

'Yes, but I only have the two prototype units. I didn't have sufficient time to manufacture more. Do you need them?'

'Yes, I believe we do. Please get them ready,' Nero replied, walking towards the rear of the Shroud's passenger compartment. Otto was sitting doodling on a pad of paper with Wing next to him, fast asleep.

'Mr Malpense, Mr Fanchu,' Nero said as he approached. Wing's eyes flicked open and immediately focused on him as Otto put the pad down on the seat next to him. It was covered in detailed electronic schematics. Nero made a mental note to get the Professor to surreptitiously have a look at the drawings. 'I know that you've both been through a lot over the last twenty-four hours, but I'm afraid there's one more thing I need you to do. I would never normally ask students to take on a mission like this but over the past couple of years you've demonstrated to me on numerous occasions that you are, quite frankly, the best infiltration team I have ever encountered. In an ideal world this is the sort of job I would give to Raven, but since she is indisposed I need to ask you if you'd be prepared to go down there and find a way into Drake's base. I'm not ordering you to do it; I'm asking you.'

'I think I speak for both of us when I say that you would have difficulty in stopping us from going down there,' Wing said.

'Good,' Nero said with a slight smile. 'All you need to do is find an entrance for the Colonel's strike team. Once the assault is under way you just keep your heads down, understood?'

'You think a direct attack is the best way?' Otto asked.

'It's the only way to ensure that Drake doesn't get the Dreadnought into the air. We have to hit them hard and hope that we can capture or disable it before that happens,' Nero explained.

'What about the people that Drake's holding hostage down there?' Otto asked, frowning.

'The plan is not without risks, Mr Malpense,' Nero said. 'We will do everything we can to get our people out safely, but we have to act swiftly and decisively. We can't afford to just wait and see what Drake will do next. The stakes are too high.'

Otto said nothing for a moment, turning over in his head the multiple different scenarios that might unfold during a full-scale armed assault on Drake's facility. 'How do we get down there undetected?' he asked after a few seconds.

'Well,' Nero said with a wry smile, 'that's where the Professor comes in.'

'You know, I was afraid you were going to say that,' Otto replied.

☢ ☢ ☢

Drake stood in the centre of the Dreadnought's bridge as his technicians completed the final pre-flight checks on its new equipment. One of his men walked across the bridge towards him, tapping away on the tablet display that he held.

'Final loadout is complete, sir,' the man said, 'and we expect to have completed new-systems testing within the next hour.'

'Excellent,' Drake said with a smile. 'I'll be in my office if anyone needs me.' He walked out of the bridge and made his way down through the maze of corridors.

Drake had to admit that it felt good to be back on board the giant aircraft. He had devoted several years of his life to its design and construction in the hopes that it would become a suitable flagship for Number One. He could still remember the pride he'd felt when he'd unveiled the Dreadnought to him and the rest of the ruling council. Just a few weeks later Number One was dead and Drake was faced with the agony of seeing Diabolus Darkdoom, a man he barely knew, take the Dreadnought as his new base of operations. It had been then that the Disciples had first approached him and explained their plan to destroy G.L.O.V.E. and replace it with a new organisation, a new organisation with Jason Drake as one of its most senior commanders. He'd needed little persuasion. Quite aside from the power that he would wield, it was the perfect opportunity to avenge Number One's death and to eliminate those responsible for his assassination. Now they were only hours away from these plans coming to fruition and the whole world being at their mercy. It felt good.

Drake walked out on to the gangway that led down from the Dreadnought and out of the hangar. He stopped halfway down and looked back at the vessel, noting with satisfaction the hatches in the underside of the hull where the new equipment had been installed. He continued down the ramp and made his way to his office. As he typed his password into his laptop three screens rose up from the desk in front of him and after a few seconds the disguised images of the other three Disciples appeared.

'We're nearly ready to launch,' Drake said with a smile. 'Everything is going according to plan.'

'Darkdoom will cooperate?' the woman on the left asked.

'Yes, he has little choice,' Drake replied. 'Capturing his son was an unexpected bonus. We always feared that he might have been prepared to sacrifice the lives of the Dreadnought's crew rather than do what we asked, but there was no way he was going to refuse when his son's life was at stake.'

'Has he been transferred to the Dreadnought yet?' the man on the centre screen asked.

'It should be happening as we speak,' Drake replied. 'His son will now be joining him, of course, to ensure his on-going cooperation. What do you want me to do with the other prisoners?'

'Execute them,' the man on the right-hand screen replied coldly. 'All of them.'

'You're sure?' Drake asked. 'They may yet be useful.'

'Quite sure,' the man replied. 'Once the Dreadnought is airborne they are surplus to requirements. They might have been useful had we managed to capture Nero but now they're just irritating loose ends. Dispose of them.'

'As you wish,' Drake said. 'Furan wishes to keep Raven alive though. He believes he can turn her.'

'He is playing with fire,' the woman said angrily. 'She is too dangerous to let her live.'

'I'm afraid I have to agree,' the man on the centre screen said. 'It's an unnecessary risk.'

'I shall inform him of your decision,' Drake replied. Furan would not be happy, but the other Disciples were right: they had enough to worry about now without any further complications.

'Good. We'll await word of the launch of the Dreadnought,' the man on the right-hand screen said and the three displays went dark.

☹☹☹

Otto stood next to Wing at the edge of the Shroud's open rear hatch as it raced across the desert at low altitude. The Professor had briefed them on the jump procedure using the new equipment and though Otto knew that he could rely on the old man's technical skills he could not ignore the fact that it was still a couple of hundred metres to the desert floor. He tried to stop thinking about the drop and just concentrate on the glowing red jump light above the hatch. A few seconds later it turned green and Wing leapt without hesitation from the hatch with Otto just a moment or two behind him.

Otto had performed a H.A.L.O. jump before, but this was quite different. In a High Altitude Low Opening parachute jump, you leapt from a plane at high altitude and opened your chute at the lowest possible altitude to lessen your chances of detection by anyone on the ground. What he and Wing were doing now was quite different and much more terrifying. This free fall lasted only a few seconds, barely giving their plummeting bodies time to reach terminal velocity. As the ground rushed up to meet Otto he couldn't help but close his eyes; every instinct screamed at him that he was about to die.

The sensors on his sophisticated suit detected that Otto was at the correct altitude to activate its systems. There was a high-pitched whine and then a massive almost subsonic, thud as the pack on Otto's back discharged. A huge concussive wave flew out from the suit, cancelling out Otto's momentum and dropping him to the floor as if he'd fallen just a couple of metres. The Professor had called it a 'localised velocity negation field' and had explained that it was derived from the same principles as the Sleeper guns that the security guards at H.I.V.E. were all issued with. All Otto really cared about at that precise moment was the fact that he wasn't a red stain in the dust of the desert floor. It had still been a jarring thud as he hit the ground on all fours, but not the bone-shattering impact it should have been. Wing landed on his feet with an agility that made it look like he'd done this a thousand times before.

'Interesting,' Wing said, walking over to Otto and offering him his hand.

'I kinda prefer skydiving with a parachute,' Otto said with a grin as Wing pulled him up. 'Call me a traditionalist.'

Otto wiped off the thin layer of dust that had already accumulated on the visor of his tactical helmet and looked around. There was nothing but sand and rocks as far as the eye could see. The only vegetation was occasional patches of dry brown scrub. It was as featureless and unwelcoming an environment as one could imagine.

Otto pulled the Blackbox PDA from one of the pouches on the front of his suit and checked the display. They were about a kilometre away from the target coordinates for the locations of the fusion cores, and the background radiation level, as it was throughout most of the test site, was unpleasantly high. That was hardly surprising considering the fact that there'd been over a hundred above-ground nuclear detonations in the area over the course of its history. Their suits offered some protection, so it probably wouldn't cause any serious long-term side effects, but they needed to get inside quickly. It was already late afternoon and it would be getting dark soon, which would make the task of finding the base even more difficult, if not impossible. Otto pointed in the direction of the suspected location of Drake's base.

'Let's go,' he said, 'before we get more than just a sun tan. Engaging active camouflage.' Otto tapped at the control panel on the wrist of his own suit. The grey and black surface of the suit instantly transitioned to a dusty brown colour that matched the colour of the desert around them. It was not the full invisibility that one of G.L.O.V.E.'s thermoptic camo suits would have offered them – the power requirements of the jump pack were too great for that – but it was the next best thing.

They set off walking through a low valley, the rocks that lined its sides carved into strange shapes, sculpted by the wind and sand. There was no sound out here, and their crunching footsteps were worryingly loud, echoing back and forth off the valley walls. Otto knew it was extremely unlikely that Drake's personnel would access the facility by land – they would be too obvious and easy to track. Far more likely instead that they were brought in by air, but if that was the case then there had to be some kind of landing area with surface access. The only problem was actually finding it.

They were now within a few hundred metres of the calculated location of the hidden facility and Otto looked around for any sign of their target. The only notable feature nearby was an enormous rocky outcropping at the top of a steep boulder-strewn slope. The area beneath it was concealed by shadow that seemed just a little *too* dark. Otto gestured to Wing and crouched down behind a nearby rock.

'Up there,' Otto said, pointing to the black hole beneath the outcropping. 'That look a little odd to you?'

'Yes, but it could just be a cave,' Wing said, examining the distant feature.

'Fancy taking a climb up there for a closer look?' Otto asked.

'Not really,' Wing replied, 'but I suspect that will make little difference.'

The pair of them crept out from behind the rock and started to scale the loose rocky surface of the slope leading up to the cave entrance. They climbed slowly and carefully, keeping the noise of their ascent to a minimum, and were halfway to the top of the slope when a figure appeared, stepping out of the darkened opening. He was wearing a white radiation protection suit and a gas mask and there was an assault rifle slung over his shoulder. Otto and Wing froze, hoping that their camouflage was good enough. The man at the cave mouth pulled off his mask and pulled down the zip on the front of his suit, reaching inside to retrieve a packet of cigarettes. Apparently the risks of environmental radiation poisoning weren't enough to keep this man from indulging his habit. Otto and Wing

181

remained motionless for several long minutes as the guard finished his cigarette and put his mask back on before wandering back into the gloom of the cave mouth.

'I believe we've found our way in,' Wing said quietly. 'Should we signal Nero?'

'No,' Otto said firmly, 'not yet.'

'Why not?' Wing asked, sounding slightly puzzled.

'Because I don't care how good Francisco's men are, if they mount a full armed assault on this place before we've freed the others, there's going to be a bloodbath and I'm not prepared to chance Nigel, Franz and the girls being caught in the crossfire,' Otto explained. 'We go in first, find and free the others and confirm that the Dreadnought is here. *Then* we call the cavalry.'

'We will be disobeying Doctor Nero's direct orders,' Wing observed.

'True,' Otto replied, 'but he did say he was asking rather than ordering . . .'

Otto continued to climb slowly and silently up the steep rock face. As he drew nearer to the mouth he could make out more details of the entrance and the white shape of the guard in the radiation suit, sitting on a boulder just inside the cave with his back to them. He didn't look like he was too concerned about the possibility of intruders and, in fairness, out here, who could blame him? Behind the guard, Otto could see a concrete landing strip leading further back into the depths of the cave. The entrance had been widened and reinforced, making it just big enough to accommodate a Shroud or a similar aircraft. This was clearly how Drake got supplies and personnel in and out, but it was obviously far too small for the Dreadnought, which meant there had to be another landing area some-where nearby.

Otto signalled to Wing, pointing at the guard and then drawing his finger across his throat. Wing nodded and carefully moved up behind the guard in complete silence. Wing tapped him on the shoulder and the guard spun around, startled. Wing ripped the gas mask off the guard's head and then pulled the white hood of the radiation suit down over his face and delivered a solid right hook to the disorientated man's chin. The guard's legs gave way beneath him and he collapsed to the floor. Wing hooked his hands under the unconscious man's armpits and quickly dragged him out of sight behind a nearby rock. Otto crept forwards and looked further into the cave. The landing strip ended at a set of heavy steel doors and, off to one side, another smaller door with a camera mounted on the wall above it. Otto ducked back behind the rocks where Wing was laying out the unconscious guard.

'Get that radiation suit off him,' Otto whispered.

☢ ☢ ☢

Laura lay on the hard concrete block that passed for one of the beds in her cell. Lucy sat on the end of the other bed while Shelby prowled back and forth across the cell near the door.

'So are they going to leave us here to rot or what?' Shelby said angrily.

'You're going to wear a groove in the floor at this rate,' Laura sighed.

'We can't just sit here and wait while they decide what they're going to do with us,' Shelby said. 'We've got to do something.'

'Like what exactly?' Laura asked.

'I dunno – dig a tunnel, take a guard hostage, something . . . anything!' Shelby snapped. She stopped pacing, took a deep breath and then sat down on the bed next to Lucy with a sigh. 'Sorry, don't mean to yell, I just can't stand being locked up like this.'

'If it's any consolation, I'm sure it's getting to all of us,' Lucy said, sounding tired.

Suddenly they heard the sound of the locks on their cell door disengaging. The door swung open and one of Drake's soldiers walked into the room.

'All of you, up against the wall.' He gestured with the muzzle of his rifle towards the wall at the far end.

Laura and Lucy got up and moved slowly towards the back of the cell. Shelby stood still, staring back at the guard.

'Don't be stupid,' the guard said, levelling the rifle at her head.

Just for a second Shelby seemed to be weighing up her chances but then she walked over and stood in silence with Laura and Lucy. The guard pointed his gun at the three of them.

'Mr Drake says goodbye,' the guard said with an evil sneer and began to squeeze the trigger. Laura tensed, inhaling sharply in fear as she realised what was about to happen.

'*Stop!*' Lucy hissed, her voice suddenly layered with what sounded like dozens of other whispered voices.

The guard froze, a look of astonishment on his face as his entire body suddenly refused to obey his unconscious instructions. Shelby and Laura looked at each other and then at the pale, slightly shocked face of Lucy. It had only been a single word but the sound was unmistakable.

'*Give me the gun,*' Lucy hissed again, holding out her hand as the guard passed her the rifle. Lucy gave it to Shelby who swung the butt into the side of the frozen guard's head, knocking him out cold as Lucy sat down heavily on the concrete bed, trembling.

'I suppose this is where I have to admit that I haven't been entirely honest with you,' she said quietly, her voice shaky. 'My name isn't really Lucy Dexter. I am Viscontessa Lucia Sinistre. My grandmother was Contessa Maria Sinistre. Perhaps I have a little explaining to do.'

chapter nine

'You can say that again,' Shelby said, staring in amazement at Lucy.

'I know. I'm sorry I lied to you all. My family history is not something I'm particularly proud of,' Lucy said with a sigh. 'I always promised myself that I would never do what I've just done. It goes against everything my mother ever taught me.'

'Your mother being the Contessa's daughter, right?' Laura asked, struggling to make sense of what she'd just seen.

'Yes, but she was the first woman in my family who didn't want to follow in her ancestors' footsteps. The women of the Sinistre family have always had this gift, if that's what you can call it, and they have always used it for their own selfish purposes. My grandmother was no exception, as you well know,' Lucy said sadly. 'Only at the end did she do anything noble and even then it cost her her life.'

'You know about that?' Laura asked. The Contessa had sacrificed her life to save everyone at H.I.V.E. from the murderous forces of Number One, but it was not exactly common knowledge outside the school.

'Doctor Nero himself told me what she did,' Lucy replied. 'I wouldn't have thought her capable of that kind of sacrifice, but perhaps I didn't know her as well as I thought. After she died, I had no one left to turn to. I spent my early life in England living with my mother, but she died several years ago and my grandmother became my legal guardian. I rarely saw her. I was kept a virtual prisoner at our family home in Italy, surrounded by my grandmother's men and educated by private tutors. It was only when my grandmother died and Doctor Nero came to me and offered me a place at H.I.V.E. that I saw a chance to escape. Perhaps it is not what my mother would have wanted for me but it is a safer place for me to be now that I have *the voice*.'

'How long have you been able to do that?' Laura gestured at the guard lying on the floor.

'For a year or so,' Lucy replied quietly. 'I had hoped that the ability might have skipped a generation, but . . .' She tailed off.

'You have it too,' Laura said as Shelby took the cuffs from the unconscious guard's belt and fastened his wrists behind his back.

'Well, it just saved our lives,' Shelby said, 'so I'm not complaining.'

'You don't understand,' Lucy said sadly. 'It's a curse. It has brought nothing but misery to my family. What do you think happens every time people discover what we can do? I'll tell you. They manipulate us to gain the power of our abilities and I fear that ultimately my grandmother was no exception. That's part of the reason I accepted Doctor Nero's offer. I need somewhere I can learn to control this skill before it can destroy me too. Ridiculous as it may sound given our current position, I thought H.I.V.E. might be the only place that was safe for me.'

'Speaking of which,' Laura said, 'now might be a good time –'

'To get the hell out of here?' Shelby offered.

'Yeah,' Laura replied, 'before this joker wakes up.' She gestured to the man on the floor of the cell.

'Any idea where we're going?' Shelby said as she took a quick peek into the corridor outside the cell door.

'Nope, we're improvising here,' Laura replied. 'First step is to see if we can find and free the others.'

'OK,' Shelby said, raising the fallen guard's rifle to her shoulder, 'let's go.'

☻☻☻

Otto walked slowly towards the door with the camera

mounted above it, his hands raised and the hard muzzle of the assault rifle pressing into the small of his back. As he got closer the door slid open and another man in a radiation suit stepped out.

'Well, look what you found,' the man said, his voice muffled by the gas mask he wore.

Wing stepped out from behind Otto and levelled the gun he was carrying at the guard.

'Please place your gun on the floor,' Wing said calmly, his voice also muffled by his mask. 'Do it now and no sudden moves, please. I would rather not have to shoot you.'

Five minutes later both the unconscious guards were safely locked in a nearby storeroom minus their radiation suits. But although Wing may have been unusually tall for a boy of his age, Otto was not and it was becoming abundantly clear that the radiation suit was not the right size for him at all.

'It is a little . . . loose,' Wing said, fighting valiantly to keep the smile from his face.

'Well, if you have any other ideas as to how we wander into this place undetected, now would be a great time to mention them,' Otto said, struggling with the oversized suit. 'And if you suggest the ventilation system I'm going to hit you.'

'I think that whoever designed this place may have

been one step ahead of us there,' Wing said, pointing to the ventilation hatch in the wall that was only ten centimetres square.

'Well, that makes a refreshing, if slightly inconvenient, change,' Otto said, zipping up the suit. 'Let's go.'

The pair of them walked along the corridor towards the elevator at the far end. As they stepped into the empty carriage Otto noted that there was a single button on the wall. This lift had just one destination and they could only hope at this point that wherever that was it wasn't swarming with heavily armed guards. He hit the button and the lift began to descend.

'I believe this is what is known as "walking into the lion's den",' Wing said.

'Yeah,' Otto said. 'The real trick, of course, is being able to walk back out again without any missing limbs.'

There was a soft ping and the elevator doors slid open. Ahead of them was a short passage with a glass wall on one side which led to a heavy door at the other end. They walked down the passage and a man who was seated behind a control console on the other side of the glass glanced up at them.

'Prepare for decontamination,' he said in a bored voice, pressing a button in front of him. Steaming liquid shot from nozzles concealed in the ceiling and sprayed Otto and Wing. They stood still as the sprays washed any stray radioactive material off the suits and after a minute or so a door ahead of them opened. Otto took this as their cue to leave and walked forwards. The bored-looking man behind the console barely looked at them. They found themselves in a room lined with hanging radiation suits identical to the ones they wore.

'I have a horrible feeling that this is where our disguises run out,' Otto said, looking at the racks of suits. He walked past them to the lockers beyond and opened one. Inside were dark grey overalls that must be what passed for a uniform inside the facility.

'It'd be nice if we could just put on these uniforms and nobody notices us,' Otto said, 'but somehow I suspect that Drake doesn't employ many people our age.'

'Yes, I fear we may draw undue attention,' Wing said with a frown.

'What we need now,' Otto said, 'is a diversion.'

☢ ☢ ☢

Raven opened her eyes as the door to her cell creaked open. She was expecting it to be Furan, come to try once again to break her, but it was not. Instead, three guards entered the room, all with their assault rifles raised and trained on her.

'On your feet,' the first guard said, waiting as she slowly stood up. She was pleased to see fear in the men's eyes.

'So you're the execution party?' Raven said. 'I'm insulted.'

'Oh really,' the first guard said, 'and why is that?'

'Because they thought three of you would be enough.'

She moved with a speed that defied belief, throwing herself forwards and rolling across the floor towards the first guard. The pain from the injuries she had sustained was gone; there was only adrenalin now. She speared upwards, swatting the barrel of the first guard's gun to one side just as he pulled the trigger. The muzzle flashed just centimetres from her head but she ignored the deafening noise and reached down to the man's waist, pulling the combat knife from his belt and with a flick of her arm sent it flying into the wrist of the second soldier, who howled in pain, his rifle falling uselessly to the floor. Her other hand smashed upwards into the first guard's chin, lifting him off his feet, out cold. The world seemed to be moving in slow motion to her now as she took two steps towards the man with the knife embedded in his wrist and, ignoring the sudden searing pain from the wound in her thigh, kicked him hard in the face, propelling him unconscious into the final guard just as he opened fire, sending his shots wild and knocking the rifle out of his hands. He collapsed under the weight of his stunned comrade and they fell in a heap of tangled limbs. Desperately, the guard threw the unconscious man from on top of him with a grunt and reached for his fallen rifle. His hand closed around the grip as Raven's booted foot smashed down on top of it, pinning it to the floor. She stood over him, the first guard's rifle in her hands and pointed straight at his head.

'Now you're going to tell me where I can find Furan,' she said, 'or I'm going to *really* get angry.'

☺ ☺ ☺

Jason Drake watched from his office as a group of guards escorted Darkdoom and his son up the gangway leading to the Dreadnought. There was a knock at the door and he called out for whoever it was to enter. Furan walked into the room.

'You wanted to see me,' Furan said.

'Yes,' Drake said, gesturing for Furan to come and join him at the window overlooking the hangar. 'I have spoken to the other Disciples and they have ordered the executions of all prisoners, including Raven. They decided she was too dangerous to spare and I have to say that I agreed with them. I know you had hoped to turn her, but under the circumstances I had no alternative but to issue an order for her execution.'

'You did what?' Furan said angrily.

'It's too late now, Pietor,' Drake said calmly. 'I gave the order ten minutes ago.'

'How many men did you send?' Furan said, an edge of panic to his voice.

'More than enough,' Drake said, frowning.

'How many?' Furan repeated quickly.

'Three,' Drake replied.

'You fool,' Furan said, shaking his head. 'You sent three men with rifles into Raven's cell. They're probably already dead. Get on board the Dreadnought and launch now.'

'I know that you respect the woman, Furan, but I think you overestimate her,' Drake replied.

'I don't just respect her, I fear her, and if you had any sense you would too.'

Suddenly the base alarm klaxon started to sound from outside.

'We leave now,' Furan said angrily, 'while we still can.'

☻ ☻ ☻

Shelby ducked back around the corner as a group of guards ran past in the opposite direction.

'Looks like they found our unconscious friend,' she whispered to Laura.

'Or something else is going on,' Laura replied.

'Whatever it is, it's got them panicked,' Lucy added. 'I doubt that will make it any easier to get out of here.'

Laura nodded. Lucy was right. They knew nothing about the layout of this facility other than what they'd seen on their way from the Dreadnought to their cell, and that was hardly going to be a viable escape route. There were occasional signs mounted on the walls of the corridor but unfortunately none of them read 'Secret Route to Hidden Exit'.

Shelby was about to look around the corner again when she heard two voices approaching down the corridor towards them.

'What's going on?' the first voice asked.

'Raven's escaped,' the second voice replied. 'There's a base-wide alert.'

'Where are you headed?'

'I have to carry out the termination order on the Argentblum kid before she makes a try for him.'

'Yeah, looks like they're tying up the loose ends. They're prepping the Dreadnought for an emergency dust-off right now.'

'OK, well I'm gonna go take care of that kid and then I'll check back in to see if there's any update on Raven's location.'

'OK. I'll see you in the hangar bay.'

The second guard headed around the corner and straight into the raised muzzle of the rifle that Shelby was holding.

'Hi,' Shelby said with a wicked smile. 'From what I've heard, lungs work a whole lot better without any holes in them. Tell you what, you take us to the "Argentblum kid" and you won't have to find that out for yourself. Deal?'

The guard just nodded, swallowing nervously.

'Which way?' Laura asked and the man nodded back down the corridor the girls had just come down. Shelby gestured with the barrel of the rifle for him to lead the way. They walked for a few minutes, stopping several times to avoid groups of guards who all seemed to be running in the opposite direction, apparently preoccupied with a much bigger threat. It didn't take a genius to work out what that threat might be. They came to a second junction and as the guard was about to walk around the corner Shelby hissed at him to stop.

'What is it?' Laura whispered.

Shelby nodded over to the far wall, where the red dots of several laser sights were moving slowly around.

'Looks like a welcoming party,' Shelby said quietly. 'I think they might be expecting a certain "crazy Russian".'

'So what do we do now?' Laura asked.

'I have an idea,' Lucy said and she walked up to the guard that Shelby was holding at gunpoint and whispered something into his ear. For a moment he almost looked confused but then he ran around the corner ahead of them and shouted to the guards who were lying in wait.

'Raven's been spotted at the other end of the base,' he yelled. 'Follow me!'

There was the sound of a commotion and then the guard that Lucy had whispered to ran off in the other direction with several men following him. Shelby cautiously peered around the corner and saw that the corridor was now clear.

'Good job,' Shelby said to Lucy. 'That's gonna come in really useful.'

'I don't know if I can do it again without some rest,' Lucy said. She looked suddenly pale and she was trembling again. 'Every time I do that I feel like my head's going to burst.'

'Don't worry,' Laura said, putting a hand on Lucy's shoulder. 'We're getting out of here and once we do you never have to use it again if you don't want to. OK?'

Lucy nodded and gave Laura a small weak smile.

'Come on,' Shelby said, 'let's go get Franz before those goons come back.'

They passed several unlocked empty offices before reaching a locked door at the far end of the corridor. Shelby quickly inspected the lock. She could shoot it out but that would make noise and draw unwanted attention and that was the last thing they needed at the moment.

'Hold this,' Shelby said, handing the rifle to Laura, who looked like she'd just been given a live rattlesnake. Shelby may have enjoyed the firearms training sessions with Colonel Francisco, but Laura had never really got used to holding what she saw as a crude machine designed to kill people.

Shelby ran back to one of the empty offices, hurried over to a desk and rummaged around inside for a few seconds before running back out of the office and down the corridor towards Laura and Lucy, straightening out a pair of paper clips with her teeth. She crouched down in front of the lock and slid the metal wires inside. Two seconds later there was a click and she opened the door. Standing against the far wall, his eyes wide with surprise, was Franz. For a moment he looked like he couldn't quite believe what he was seeing and then he ran across the room and engulfed Shelby in a crushing bear hug.

'Shelby!' he cried as he hugged her. He moved to Laura and hugged her too. 'Laura!' he exclaimed happily and released her before embracing a slightly startled-looking Lucy. 'New girl whose name I am not quite remembering!' he said happily.

'Lucy,' she gasped as he hugged her.

'Yes, of course, Lucy.' Franz released her and gave all three of the girls a beaming smile. 'I am knowing that someone would be rescuing me. I was not sure who – perhaps Raven, perhaps Doctor Nero, perhaps even Otto and Wing. But being rescued by you is a lovely surprise! I would never have been expecting the girls to be doing the heroic rescuings.' His voice had a certain manic tone to it, which Laura guessed must be down to a combination of exhaustion, delayed shock and adrenalin.

'Erm . . . thanks. I think,' Laura said, noting the look of irritation on Shelby's face.

'Quickly now,' Franz said, hurrying past them into the corridor. 'They have taken Nigel but I have a plan for the rescuing and we must act swiftly. Do not worry, I will lead the way. On the way here I am memorising the route. You have done your part but now is being the time for action!'

'Give me the gun,' Shelby whispered to Laura as Franz rushed off down the corridor.

'Why?' Laura asked.

'Because if he carries on like that, I'm gonna have to shoot him.'

☢ ☢ ☢

'You have to clear this area now!' the shorter of the two men in radiation suits yelled as he ran towards the guard. His companion was waving a small black device around that was emitting a high-pitched beeping sound.

'What's going on?' the guard demanded.

'Someone's flooded this area with radioactive gas from the fusion core,' the figure in the radiation suit said urgently. 'We have to get everyone out of here.'

'Radioactive gas?' the guard said, sounding suddenly nervous.

'Yes,' the man in the radiation suit said, 'colourless, odourless and quite, quite deadly. How are the levels?' he asked, turning to his companion. The other man showed him the display on the small black device and the first man shook his head. 'Good God, she'll kill us all.'

'Mr Drake said I wasn't to leave my station or let anyone leave this room under any circumstances,' the guard said nervously, glancing up at the air vents in the ceiling.

'You see, this is what I admire,' the man in the radiation suit said to his companion, slapping the guard on the shoulder, 'a man whose loyalty to his employer outweighs his fear of a slow, lingering, painful death. Such courage.'

'Erm . . . perhaps you're right though,' the guard said quickly. 'Perhaps we should evacuate. Just to be on the safe side. How long do we have?'

'Well, if your gums aren't bleeding yet then you've probably got . . . oh . . . two or three minutes to get everyone out of this area,' the man in the suit said.

The guard swallowed nervously and quickly punched a code into the numerical keypad next to the door and opened it before rushing into the room behind. A few seconds later a group of frightened-looking people dashed out of the room, followed by the guard. He went to close the door but the man in the suit stopped him.

'No, I need to check the . . . errr . . . the levels,' the man in the suit said.

'Yes,' the other man said, 'the levels. It's very important.'

The guard looked at them both curiously. The first man suddenly reached up and brushed something off the guard's shoulder.

'Sorry,' he said, 'you've just got some hair falling out there.'

'Right,' the guard said quickly, the look of suspicion replaced by fear, 'I'll leave you to it.' He ran off down the corridor like he was being chased by a pack of wild dogs.

The two men in the radiation suits walked into the launch control centre and closed the door behind them. Otto pulled off his gas mask and pulled down the elasti-cated white hood of his suit.

'"It'll never work, Otto,"' he said as he unzipped the front of the suit. '"He'll never believe you, Otto."'

'OK, OK,' Wing said as he pulled off his mask too. 'Remind me never again to underestimate your capacity for deceit.'

'Ye of little faith,' Otto said with a grin. 'Personally I blame the education of henchmen these days. Everyone knows that regardless of whether it's a tokamak or laser-pellet-type fusion reactor, it still doesn't produce radiation levels higher than standard background.'

'Oh yes,' Wing replied with a slight smile, 'everyone knows that.'

Otto walked over to one of the consoles that were arrayed beneath the large window that looked out into the Dreadnought's hangar bay. He placed his hand on one of the control panels and closed his eyes.

'Now let's see if we can't open this sucker up,' he whispered.

☢ ☢ ☢

'I think we have something here,' Professor Pike said.

Dr Nero and Colonel Francisco hurried over to where the Professor was staring at the live satellite feed on his laptop. He pointed at the screen, where a thin white line was widening into a rectangle in the middle of the darkened desert floor. As more light flooded out of the illuminated hole the distinctive outline of the Dreadnought slowly became visible.

'Have we heard anything from Otto or Wing yet?' Nero asked. The Colonel shook his head. 'Very well. Colonel, prep your men to drop,' Nero said quickly.

'Yes, sir,' the Colonel replied.

☢ ☢ ☢

Raven kicked in the door of Furan's quarters, rifle raised. The room was empty, just as she had suspected it would be, but it was the only place that the terrified guard had been able to come up with. She turned to leave when something caught her eye. Lying on top of Furan's desk was a pair of familiar scabbards. Raven walked across the room and pulled one of the katanas from its sheath, the edge crackling with a dark purple energy field that gave the swords a cutting edge quite unlike any other weapon on earth. She quickly fastened the swords across her back, one hilt behind each shoulder and smiled.

'Now we're really back in business,' she said to herself.

She headed towards the door but stopped short when she heard running footsteps coming down the corridor outside. Silently Raven drew the swords from her back and waited until the sound got nearer before springing into the corridor, weapons raised.

'Aaaarrrggghh!' Franz screamed in terror.

Raven lowered her weapons, smiling as Laura, Shelby and Lucy came running up behind him.

'Sorry,' Raven said, putting the katanas back in their scabbards, 'I didn't mean to startle you.'

'I am thinking that the new underwear might be being needed sooner rather than later,' Franz said plaintively.

'Eeeww. So much more information than necessary,' Shelby said with a grimace.

'It's nice to see a friendly face,' Lucy said. 'Any idea how we get out of this place?'

'No,' Raven replied, 'other than the way we came in, but I don't think that's going to be easy. Anyway, we still have to find Diabolus and Nigel. We're not leaving the Darkdooms behind.'

'They have been taken to the Dreadnought,' Franz said quickly. 'Nigel was locked up with me but then they took him away. I heard one of the guards saying that they were taking him to the ship. Nigel told me they had already used him to make his father do things that he was not wanting to. I am thinking that they will be doing the same thing now, ja?'

'Whatever their plan is, we have to stop it before –'

'This is Furan,' a voice suddenly came over the speakers mounted in the corridor ceiling. 'We have a facility breach. All security teams report to the Dreadnought hangar immediately.'

'Sounds like someone else is breaking out,' Laura said.

'Or perhaps breaking in,' Raven said with a slight smile.

☹ ☹ ☹

Otto opened his eyes and looked out through the window into the hangar. The huge doors overhead were slowly sliding apart and through the widening gap he could see the dark early evening sky. His attention was caught by a commotion on the gangway leading up to the Dreadnought as Nigel, Darkdoom and two other men were escorted up the ramp by a squad of soldiers. Otto had not seen the two men with Nigel before but he recognised one of them from the photo he had seen above the reception desk of the Drake Industries building in New York. It was Jason Drake. What did he need Nigel for? And where were the rest of their friends? He wasn't sure if the fact that they weren't with Drake was a good thing or not.

'We have to get on board the Dreadnought and stop it from launching,' Otto said to Wing.

'You can't do that from here?' Wing asked, looking slightly puzzled. This room was, after all, the launch control.

'I tried to while I was inside the network,' Otto said, shaking his head, 'but the systems that control the launch procedures have all had their control routines transferred to the Dreadnought and they're completely blocked from external access. I might be able to get through the firewall if I had Laura's help, but at the moment the only way to stop that thing from getting into the air is to get on board and access the systems directly.'

'That is unfortunate,' Wing said, gesturing to the large concentration of Drake's guards that were fortifying the position around the base of the boarding ramp. 'I can't imagine they will be keen to welcome us on board.'

'Yes, you're probably right,' Otto said with a frown, 'but there has to be another way to get inside that thing.' He looked around the hangar searching for any vulnerability, something that Drake and his guards wouldn't expect.

Suddenly an idea formed in his head.

'Come on,' Otto said, gesturing for Wing to follow him as he ran out of the room.

☢ ☢ ☢

The two cloaked Shrouds touched down on the desert floor in a cloud of dust and two portals of light opened as their loading ramps descended. Francisco's men poured out and headed for the huge, brightly lit hole in the desert floor. From below could be heard the sound of distant alarm bells ringing combined with the slowly escalating whining roar of the Dreadnought's giant engines spinning up.

Francisco gestured for his men to spread out along the edge of the opening and prepare to descend. As he reached the edge he fired the grappler bolt into the ground and barely hesitated before leaping over the edge, the mono-filament cable taking his weight as he plummeted into the hangar, the reel mechanism in the small of his back whining as it spooled out the line. All around him his men, dressed in suits of flexible black body armour, followed his lead, dropping into the cavern like a swarm of spiders descending from their webs.

As he dropped quickly towards the hangar floor, Francisco picked out a target, one of Drake's guards, shouldered his weapon and fired. Quickly all hell broke loose as the two opposing forces engaged with one another. Francisco's men scattered for cover as they landed on the hangar floor, bullets pinging off the concrete around them.

'Pick your targets and watch your background!' Francisco yelled as the firefight blazed. 'We have friendlies down here, remember.' These men were well trained and highly disciplined but he didn't want any accidents.

Up on the gangway, Drake hurried inside the Dreadnought, the main hatch sliding shut moments after he passed through.

'Who the hell opened the hangar doors?' Drake demanded as he stormed down the corridor leading to the bridge.

'Somebody accessed the systems in the launch control room after it was evacuated in error,' Furan said, listening to the panicked chatter that was coming in from across the facility over his headset.

'Evacuated!' Drake yelled angrily. 'I gave orders that it was to be protected at all costs. Why was it evacuated?'

'It's not entirely clear,' Furan replied. 'Something to do with a radiation leak.'

'Am I surrounded by cretins?' Drake spat. 'The only radiation around here is up there.' He gestured upwards to the desert overhead. He and Furan strode on to the bridge and headed over to the primary flight controls.

'Are we ready to launch?' Drake demanded angrily.

'Engines are starting up, sir,' the uniformed helmsman responded. 'Three minutes till launch.'

'Cloaking field?' Drake asked the tactical officer.

'Charging, sir. We're not quite ready yet. Launch wasn't scheduled for another twenty minutes.'

'Yes, well, the small army of heavily armed H.I.V.E. soldiers that just invaded the hangar forced us to move the timetable ahead a little,' Drake said angrily, 'so get the damn cloak online now!'

'Starting to feel like everything's falling apart yet, Jason?' Darkdoom said from the other side of the bridge, where he stood handcuffed and flanked by armed guards.

'I suggest you hold your tongue, Darkdoom, before I decide to throw you overboard once we're airborne,' Drake snapped back.

'You're not going to do that,' Darkdoom said. 'You need me for something. If you didn't I'd be dead already.'

'We may need you now, Darkdoom,' Furan said, walking over to him and putting his face just centimetres away from Darkdoom's, 'but soon you'll have outworn your usefulness and then I'm going to kill you very, very slowly, but not before I've made you watch me do the same thing to your son.'

Darkdoom said nothing, just stared back at him with a

look of undisguised hatred and contempt.

☢ ☢ ☢

'I assume you know where we're going,' Wing said as he
and Otto ran up the stairs.

'I got the schematics of this place while I was
connected to the network,' Otto replied, 'trust me.'

The stairs were deserted, just as the corridors they'd run
through to get there had been. The base personnel were
either taking shelter somewhere or were engaged in the
raging battle that could be heard going on in the distance.
The cavalry had clearly arrived but Otto knew that they
weren't going to be able to stop the Dreadnought
launching now. That was up to him and Wing.

They reached the top of the stairs and found a steel
hatch with a large wheel in the centre of it. Wing spun
the wheel, disengaging the heavy bolts that held it in
place, and swung it open. Suddenly the noise of the battle
in the hangar bay was much louder. Otto peered out
through the hatch and could see a narrow catwalk that led
out to a crane mounted on the ceiling of the hangar. Far
below he could see the muzzle flashes of the two sides
engaged in fierce combat. Drake's men had the advantage
of elevation but the H.I.V.E. soldiers were slowly pushing
towards the metal stairs that led up from the hangar floor
to the Dreadnought's loading ramp.

'Come on,' Otto said, gesturing for Wing to follow him out on to the narrow catwalk and towards the crane.

They made their way slowly along the long boom arm that extended out over the aft superstructure of the Dreadnought.

'Ready?' Otto asked Wing.

Wing nodded and punched one of the buttons on the wrist control panel of his dropsuit. Otto did the same, just as a horrible thought crossed his mind.

'Did Professor Pike mention to you if these things had enough charge for more than one drop?' Otto shouted over the increasing roar of the Dreadnought's engines.

'No,' Wing yelled in reply, 'but there is, as they say, one sure-fire way to find out.' He stepped off the crane and fell towards the Dreadnought's deck just as the enormous aircraft began to lift from its landing supports. Otto took a deep breath and let go of the crane too. He plummeted towards the rising Dreadnought, holding his breath the whole way down.

☣ ☣ ☣

Francisco cursed aloud as the Dreadnought started to rise into the air, the downdraught from the clusters of giant turbine engines filling the hangar with swirling hurricane-strength winds just as the last of Drake's men fell. Francisco and his men had almost made it to the end of the boarding ramp but they had not been able to fight past the last few remaining guards quickly enough. There was nothing they could do now to stop the giant vessel from launching; certainly none of the light weaponry they were equipped with would even make a dent in the thing's armoured hull.

There were a couple of cries of surprise from behind him and Francisco turned just in time to see Raven sprint past. She drew the swords from her back as she ran up the boarding ramp, past the fallen bodies of Drake's guards, and leapt off it straight towards the flat armoured hull of the Dreadnought as it rose up in front of her. With an aggressive yell she thrust both of the swords into the armour of the giant aircraft. The adaptive forcefields that made up their blades sharpened to a mono-molecular edge that slid into the toughened steel like it was cardboard. She clung desperately to the hilts of the katanas, ignoring the protests of her battered body as the ground dropped away beneath her.

Back on the gangway below Francisco watched, powerless to do anything, as the Dreadnought rose up through the giant opening overhead and climbed into the night sky.

'Colonel!' one of his men shouted from behind him and he turned to see Laura, Shelby, Lucy and Franz standing in the doorway leading back into the facility, looking tired and a bit dishevelled, but otherwise intact.

'Well, that's something at least,' Francisco said.

Suddenly a computerised voice came from the speakers in the corridor.

'Facility self-destruct sequence initiated. Time to detonation: five minutes and counting.'

'Oh, this just keeps getting better and better,' Shelby said with a sigh.

chapter ten

Dr Nero watched from the cockpit of one of the cloaked Shrouds as the Dreadnought rose up above the desert floor and into the sky. He cursed quietly under his breath. 'Can we follow it?' he asked the pilot.

'Yes, sir,' the pilot replied, 'but only until he engages the cloaking . . .'

As if in response to the pilot's words the outline of the Dreadnought flickered then faded from view as its thermoptic camouflage systems engaged.

'Anything?' Nero asked the Professor who was sitting at the control panel at the rear of the cockpit, analysing the Shroud's sensor readings.

'No, nothing,' the Professor said matter of factly. 'Its stealth systems are as efficient as the Shroud's. I'm afraid that the Dreadnought is now, to all intents and purposes, invisible. Hold on a second . . .'

'What is it?' Nero demanded, his patience now worn

well and truly thin.

'I'm picking up the transponders from Malpense and Fanchu's dropsuits heading away from here at considerable speed.'

'They're on board?' Nero asked quickly. 'Can we track them?'

'Yes, it would appear so,' the Professor replied happily, 'as long as we stay within range, that is. About fifteen kilometres or so.'

'Right, feed their coordinates to navigation,' Nero said. 'We have to keep up with them.'

'No problem sir,' the pilot said and pushed the throttle forward.

'This is Colonel Francisco to Doctor Nero, come in please, Doctor Nero,' the Colonel's voice crackled over the cockpit radio.

'This is Nero,' he said, picking up the handset and speaking into it, 'go ahead, Colonel.'

'I need both the Shrouds down here now, Max. Drake has activated a self-destruct mechanism with a five-minute timer and I've got all of my people and the Dreadnought's original crew to evacuate.'

Nero felt the frustration build up inside him like lava in a volcano. If he broke off pursuit of the Dreadnought now they'd have no chance of finding it again, but if he didn't he'd be leaving some of his people to die.

'Roger that, Colonel,' Nero said. He put the handset down and spoke to the pilot. 'Turn us around and signal the other Shroud to land with us inside the Dreadnought hangar.'

'Yes, sir,' the pilot replied and banked the Shroud around hard to the left, back towards Drake's base.

'Damn it!' Nero yelled and punched the bulkhead next to him hard enough to make his knuckles bleed.

☢ ☢ ☢

Laura sat down at the terminal on the desk in Drake's recently abandoned office and started to type.

'Three minutes till detonation,' the synthesised voice said.

'Why do that?' Shelby asked.

'Do what?' Laura said, sounding distracted.

'Have a timer on your self-destruct device,' Shelby said. 'Why not just let the Dreadnought get clear of the hangar bay and then BOOM!'

'It is kind of traditional,' Laura said, her fingers flying over the keyboard.

'Not to mention dramatic,' Lucy said.

'Anything yet?' Francisco asked as he strode into the office.

'Working on it, Colonel,' Laura said quickly, 'but the security's pretty tight here.'

The Colonel watched through a large window looking out on to the hangar bay as the two Shrouds uncloaked and landed in the middle of the cavernous space.

'OK, there's good news, bad news and worse news,' Laura said, staring at the screen and looking slightly pale.

'The good news?' Francisco asked.

'I've worked out why there was a five-minute timer on the self-destruct system,' Laura said.

'Go on,' the Colonel said, frowning slightly.

'Because five minutes is just enough time to get to minimum safe distance,' Laura replied.

'Safe distance from what?' Shelby asked nervously.

'The detonation of the one-megaton nuclear device buried under the hangar floor,' Laura said, swallowing nervously.

'There's worse news than that?' Lucy asked.

'Yeah,' Laura said quietly, 'I can't stop it.'

'This is the Colonel,' Francisco said quickly into his headset microphone, 'all teams are to board the Shrouds now and prepare for emergency dust-off. Get the first one off the ground ASAP. There's a nuke under our feet and no way to defuse it in time.'

The Professor's voice replied, 'How large a device is it, Colonel?'

'Two minutes till detonation,' the synthesised voice reported calmly.

'Miss Brand informs me that it's a one-megaton bomb,' the Colonel replied, 'and that she doesn't think she can stop it from going off.'

'With a device that size there's really no purpose in running at this point, Colonel. Let me speak to her,' the Professor said and Francisco pulled off his headset and handed it to Laura.

'Make it quick,' Laura said as she put the headset on.

'Laura, it's Professor Pike, are you quite certain about the nature of the device?' he asked.

'Yes,' Laura said, 'the specs are all here. If I had an hour or two I might be able to disarm it remotely but there's not enough time.'

'Then we need to make more,' the Professor said. 'The device is probably slaved to the central network . . .'

'The system clock,' Laura said quickly, 'of course.'

Her fingers started to fly over the keyboard again as she searched the network for the routines she needed. She found what she was looking for and opened a connection to the internet. She typed in the address of the site that she had memorised years before and silently prayed that the file she'd left was still there.

'One minute till detonation,' the computerised voice warned.

'Gotcha,' Laura whispered, opening the file.

'Warning! This is an executable file and may contain

harmful programs,' the window that popped up on Laura's screen said.

'You'd better believe it,' Laura whispered to the computer and hit the 'Open' button. She waited anxiously as the seconds ticked past.

'Thirty seconds till detonation.'

'Is it working?' Shelby asked.

'I'll let you know in thirty seconds,' Laura replied.

'Twenty seconds till detonation.'

Everyone in the room fell silent. There was nothing more they could do now.

'Ten . . . nine . . . eight . . . seven . . . seven . . . seven . . .'

Laura looked at the screen. A new window had popped up and then another and another, filling the screen with cascades of error messages.

'Catastrophic viral intrusion detected,' the computerised voice reported. 'Initiating system restore and reboot.'

'GO!' Laura yelled, leaping up from behind the desk and sprinting for the door with the others right behind her. She dashed down the stairs leading to the hangar floor, taking them two at a time.

'How long have we got?' Lucy yelled as they ran.

'I have no idea,' Laura replied honestly.

They sprinted up the loading ramp at the rear of the

nearest Shroud and it began to lift off immediately, the ramp closing as it rose out of the hangar.

'I wonder if any of Drake's people are still down there,' Laura said as she strapped herself into one of the seats that lined the wall of the bay.

'Definitely falls under "not my problem" at the moment, I'm afraid,' Shelby said as the Shroud's engines roared.

Up in the cockpit Nero watched the navigation display nervously as it showed their range from Drake's base.

'Three kilometres out and counting,' he said.

'We're red-lined,' the pilot reported, holding the control stick tightly as the Shroud's engines reached their maximum output.

'Five kilometres.'

The engines screamed, the airframe groaning in protest at being pushed to its structural limits.

'Six kilometres,' Nero said, bracing himself against the bulkhead.

'Coming up on minimum safe distance,' the Professor reported from behind him.

Suddenly the cockpit lit up like it was daytime with a searing bright double flash.

'Brace for impact,' the Professor yelled.

Moments later the shock wave hit and the pilot fought desperately with the controls, trying to keep the bucking dropship in the air. After a few seconds the wave had passed, the turbulence stopped and the pilot brought the Shroud back under control.

'I think I'd describe that as uncomfortably close,' the Professor said.

'And I think I might describe that as an understatement,' Nero said, letting out a long deep breath.

Nero climbed down the ladder into the cargo area. Between Francisco's men and the original crew of the Dreadnought that were squeezed on board there was little room to move. He made his way through the crowded passenger compartment until he found the Colonel, who was checking on one of his injured men.

'How are our losses?' Nero asked.

'It could have been worse,' Francisco replied, 'a lot worse.' He nodded his head towards Laura, who was sitting with her eyes closed and the back of her head resting against the wall between Shelby and Lucy.

'Ladies,' Dr Nero said as he approached and Laura's eyes flicked open, 'I'm glad to see that you're all safe. When I learnt of your capture by Jason Drake I feared the worst. Mercifully my fears were unfounded. Miss Brand, you averted potential disaster. You have my thanks – you saved us all.'

'Thank you, sir,' Laura said. 'Are Otto and Wing safe?'

'As far as we know they're alive,' Nero replied with a

slight frown, 'but I think it might be a little optimistic to say that they're safe. They're on board the Dreadnought.'

'What?' Shelby asked. 'How were they captured?'

'Oh, they weren't captured,' Nero replied. 'In fact, I believe it would be more accurate to say that they stowed away.'

☻ ☻ ☻

Otto and Wing slowly and carefully made their way down the external walkway running along the starboard side of the Dreadnought, the wind constantly threatening to pluck them from the precarious platform as the giant aircraft climbed higher and higher into the sky. It was pointless trying to talk; the howling gale would have made them inaudible to each other. Worse than that, at this altitude the air was already starting to get thinner and it was bitterly cold. Otto knew that they had to get inside soon, before they started to suffer from oxygen deprivation or exposure. He stopped for a moment and pointed ahead of them to a hatch at the far end of the walkway. Wing nodded and they continued edging painstakingly towards the entrance.

As they reached the hatch there was a bright double flash that illuminated the Dreadnought's superstructure like daylight. At first Otto thought it was lightning, but then Wing tugged on his arm and Otto turned around. Many kilometres behind them a giant fireball was rising from the desert floor, creating a distinctive mushroom-shaped cloud. It was beautiful and terrifying all at the same time. There could be little doubt that it had come from the location of Drake's secret facility and Otto silently prayed that the others were safe. He pushed that thought to the back of his mind, and turned back to focus on the locking mechanism of the hatch. Compared to some of the other machines that he'd had to interface with over the past couple of days, this one was comparatively straightforward. All he had to do was convince it that it really, really wanted to be unlocked right now. A moment later a green light came on above the door and it slid open. Otto pulled himself inside and then helped Wing through before hitting the switch inside to reseal the hatch. They found themselves in a dimly illuminated steel-lined corridor.

'Come on,' Otto said, 'we need to find somewhere to hole up. You can bet that hatch opening has just set all sorts of alarms buzzing up on the bridge. We're going to have company any minute now.'

They both crept away down the corridor, hoping to find somewhere they could lie low for a while. Nigel was somewhere on board this thing and there would be nothing they could do to help him if they were locked up in a holding cell somewhere.

☹ ☹ ☹

The flash lit up the bridge for an instant.

'Confirming detonation of self-destruct device,' one of the bridge officers reported to Drake.

'Excellent,' Drake said with a smile. That was another loose end taken care of. After they had completed their mission there would be no need for somewhere to hide the Dreadnought.

'I've got a couple of odd readings here,' the security chief said, looking at the screen in front of him with a frown. 'One of the external hatches just opened for a few seconds. Probably a glitch, but I'm going to send a team to investigate anyway. The other thing is a pressure leak on one of the engineering decks. It could be another error or it could just be some minor damage to the hull that we picked up during the battle in the hangar. I'll get engineering to send someone down there just in case.'

'Very well,' Drake replied. 'Keep me updated.' He was not entirely surprised that the Dreadnought was experiencing the occasional glitch; they had, after all, carried out some fairly major modifications over the past couple of days. 'I'm going to my quarters for a short while,' he said, standing up from his command seat. 'Inform me immediately if you encounter any further problems.'

Drake walked off the bridge and down the short corridor that led to his private quarters. A tiny retinal scanner above the door flashed as it confirmed his identity. Once inside, he sat down at his desk. Drake had ordered that Darkdoom's possessions be destroyed and replaced with his own. Now that Number One was gone, this was his ship and he didn't want to be reminded of the fact that any other man had commanded it, even if it had only been for a short time.

There was a beep from the console on Drake's desk and he pressed a button to respond.

'Yes, what is it?' he asked impatiently.

'We have a transmission coming in on your secured channel, sir. Would you like to receive it?'

Drake sighed. He had been expecting this. Better to get it out of the way now.

'Put it through,' he replied and leant back in his chair. The large widescreen display on his desk split into three sections and in each appeared the distorted face of one of the three Disciples.

'Good evening,' Drake said cordially, 'what can I do for you all?'

'You can begin by explaining why there has just been a thermonuclear explosion at your facility in Nevada,' the woman on the left-hand side snapped.

'G.L.O.V.E. forces attacked the facility,' Drake replied. 'I took the decision to ensure that they would never be able to retrieve anything of use from the site.'

'A somewhat extreme solution to the problem,' the man on the right said. 'The Americans are going frantic. The public are being told that it was an unscheduled nuclear test and that it's nothing to worry about. At least the location of your base allows them to use that as a plausible cover story, but behind the scenes the security forces are on high alert.'

'Not only that, but you know how jumpy unscheduled nuclear tests make the Russians and Chinese. It has made an already complex situation even more difficult,' the other man explained.

'I think we should all maintain a sense of perspective,' Drake said. 'In a few hours it won't matter what the Americans are doing and our friends in Russia and China will have far bigger problems to contend with.'

'The target has not diverted?' the woman asked.

'No, why would it?' Drake replied. 'If anything it will mean that the target is viable for longer if a state of emergency has been quietly declared by the US intelligence services.'

'Even so,' the man in the centre said, 'I think we would all rather any unscheduled improvisation be kept to a minimum for the rest of the day.'

'You can't make an omelette without breaking a few eggs,' Drake said with a smile.

'I would hardly classify a one-megaton nuclear detonation

as a broken egg, Mr Drake,' the woman replied.

'I'll contact you when the target has been intercepted,' Drake said impatiently. 'Drake out.'

He hit the button on the console and settled back in his seat, frowning. He was beginning to wonder if the Disciples were as far-sighted as he was. They seemed to have embraced his plan but he didn't know if they would have the nerve to carry through with what had to be done. Did he really need them once the plan was in motion? After all, one could not rule the world by committee.

☢ ☢ ☢

Otto and Wing crouched at the back of the power-distribution junction, hiding behind one of the humming transformers that filled the room, barely daring to breathe as the guard swept the beam of his torch back and forth. Seemingly satisfied, he closed the door again, plunging the room back into barely illuminated gloom, just a single dim light in the centre of the ceiling still burning.

'I'm getting really sick of sneaking around,' Otto said, leaning back against the wall.

'Perhaps we should just go and ask Mr Drake if he is prepared to hand Nigel and his father over to us,' Wing said, raising an eyebrow. 'He seems such a reasonable man.'

'You do know that sarcasm is the lowest form of wit,

right?' Otto asked with a smile.

'I thought it was funny pictures of kittens from the internet,' Wing said with a straight face.

'OK, that's the lowest form of wit but just above that is sarcasm,' Otto replied. 'Now perhaps we should concentrate on finding Nigel.'

'Indeed,' Wing said with a nod. 'Can you detect anything from the Dreadnought's network?'

'No, I need to get nearer to an access point. I can feel the control sub-systems all around us but there's no way into the central network from here.'

'So where do we find such an access point?' Wing asked.

'I'm not sure,' Otto said, thinking back to the limited tour that Darkdoom had given them of the Dreadnought just a couple of days earlier. It already seemed like weeks ago. 'I suppose the best bet is to head towards the bridge, but that's going to be the most secure location on the ship. It won't be easy.'

'When is it ever?' Wing asked with a tiny smile.

'I know,' Otto replied, 'but just once it might be nice, you know.'

☙ ☙ ☙

The technician headed towards the area of the engineering deck where the bridge had recorded a pressure drop. The pressure doors at the end of the passageway, where the leak was located, had sealed shut automatically, just as they were supposed to do. It looked like it was more than just a glitch after all. He sighed and slipped on the oxygen mask attached to the tank on his back before punching the override code into the pad on the wall to open the hatch. As soon as the door opened, air rushed in, trying to escape from the pressurised interior to the outside. He clipped his safety line on to the bracket next to the door and headed inside.

'Jeez,' the man whispered into his mask as he saw the true extent of the damage to the outer hull. He'd been expecting a bullet hole maybe, or a small shrapnel puncture, but this was a neat, almost circular hole about half a metre in diameter. It looked for all the world like something had sliced through the hull, but the edges weren't molten as he would have expected with someone using a cutting torch; they were smooth.

The man gasped as an arm wrapped around his neck from behind, pressing against his windpipe, making it difficult for him to breath. He felt something hard and sharp press into his side and immediately scrapped any idea he might have had of offering resistance to whomever had hold of him. His assailant turned him back towards the door and he dutifully opened it. As soon as they passed through the door he was pushed forward and he fell on to all fours, rolling on to his back and scrambling away backwards as his attacker hit the button to reseal the pressure hatch. He gasped as the woman stepped forward into the light. She took a long deep breath and looked down at him.

'Not much oxygen up here,' she said, her Russian accent unmistakable. 'Haven't had to do that for a while.'

She stepped towards him, sliding the sword with the strangely glowing blade that she'd been holding against his ribs back into one of the crossed scabbards on her back.

'I'm sorry, allow me to introduce myself. My name is Raven,' she said. 'You've probably heard stories about me. Let me assure you that most of them are true.' She took a single step towards him, a terrifying predatory smile on her face. 'Now, tell me where I can find Darkdoom and his son or I'll have to prove it to you.'

☢ ☢ ☢

Otto crept down the corridor behind Wing. They were getting nearer to the bridge now and still he couldn't sense the Dreadnought's central network. It was strange, because when Darkdoom had been showing them around the ship, Otto had been able to feel the low-level buzz of the computer core that controlled the giant vessel from much further away.

'Anything?' Wing whispered, listening for the sound of anyone approaching their position.

'No and I don't understand why not,' Otto said. It was almost like there was a dead spot where the data stream should be, like a living healthy body with no heartbeat. It made no sense. He suddenly remembered the last time he'd felt anything like that. He'd been on an automated train speeding through the Alps that had been equipped with a new system, an organic supercomputer that had been immune to his control.

'Wait!' Otto whispered urgently and looked up at the corridor ceiling. 'Give me a leg up.'

Wing moved over to Otto and crouched down, lacing his fingers. Otto put one foot in his friend's hands and Wing lifted him up towards the ceiling. He pulled a panel off the cable trunking that ran along the top of the wall and looked inside. There, interwoven with the normal cabling, was a slimy black web that looked for all the world like the veins of some hideous creature's circulatory system. Otto went to touch one of the tendrils, but before he could the tendril whipped out towards his outstretched finger. Otto recoiled, snatching his hand back before the thing could touch him, and leapt down to the floor again. The tendril that had reached for Otto snaked back inside the thick bunches of normal cabling that ran through the trunking.

Otto's mind raced. When they'd first encountered this stuff it had been inert, not capable of moving in the way it just had. This was an evolution of that technology but, even more worryingly, it meant that Drake must be somehow involved in its development.

'What is it?' Wing said, noting Otto's shocked expression.

'Something really bad,' Otto said. 'I'll explain later. Forget the access points. We just need to find Darkdoom and Nigel and get off this ship.'

☹ ☹ ☹

'Report!' Drake ordered as he walked back on to the bridge.

'Target is 1.5 kilometres out, sir,' the tactical officer reported.

'And they have no idea we're here?' Drake asked.

'No, sir,' the man replied. 'Cloaking systems are functioning perfectly. There is no indication they have detected us. The escorts are still in formation.'

'Communications jamming?'

'Ready, sir,' a woman sat at another station reported.

'Weapons?'

'Locked and tracking, sir!'

'Very good,' Drake said with a smile. 'Let us begin.'

☹ ☹ ☹

Colonel Matthew Woods was a thirty-year man – thirty years service in the United States Air Force and he knew that, like the type of plane he currently flew, he was nearing the end of his working life. He couldn't complain; he'd had as good a career as an air force pilot could hope for and the job didn't get much more glamorous than the seat he was currently sitting in. He couldn't honestly say it was exciting work, but it was certainly satisfying.

'What the hell is that?' his co-pilot said and Woods looked up from the flight plan he'd been studying. He had more flight time logged than almost any other pilot he knew but he'd never seen anything like this before. Ahead of them a boiling black storm front was blossoming into existence out of thin air. It was exactly the type of cloud that no pilot in his right mind would ever dream of trying to fly through.

'Where the hell did that come from?' Woods asked. They'd have to go around it; there was certainly no way through it. He pushed at his flight controls and the giant aircraft slowly banked to the left. As it turned, the storm clouds seemed to spread across the sky, blocking their path. It was uncanny.

'Call it in,' Woods said.

'I got nothing,' the flight engineer sat behind him reported. 'Comms are down. I can't even raise the escorts.'

Woods looked out over the plane's port wing at the

F-22 fighter that was flying alongside. He wondered if they were experiencing the same problems.

'Reboot the comms systems,' Woods ordered. 'Could be the hardware.'

Suddenly he felt turbulence shaking the control yoke in his hands.

'Now what?' he asked. He started at the sound and feeling of a jarring thud as something impacted the top of the aircraft. He pushed at the controls but they did not respond. Both of the F-22s flying escort broke violently away from Woods' wing tips as something enormous, surely much too large to be another aircraft, just seemed to appear from thin air overhead.

'Sweet Mary, mother of God,' he whispered. He watched in horror as multiple white missile trails raced across the sky, converging with both escort fighters and turning them into blazing balls of tumbling debris before their pilots even had time to react. Knowing that no one would probably hear the transmission but aware that he had to make it anyway, he thumbed his radio control and spoke.

'Mayday, Mayday, this is Air Force One, we are under attack, repeat, we are under attack.'

chapter eleven

'Docking clamps locked in position,' Drake's tactical officer reported.

'Escort fighters neutralised.'

'Flight systems interface complete. Controls locked out. She's ours, sir.'

Drake smiled. It had gone just as smoothly as he had hoped it would. It was hardly the sort of attack that the Americans could possibly have predicted; they had been caught unaware and unprepared, just as he had planned.

'The Zeus Sphere?' Drake asked.

'Functioning perfectly, sir. We are storm-cloaked,' the chief engineer reported. 'As far as any satellite surveillance is concerned, Air Force One just disappeared in one of the worst storms that the Atlantic has ever seen. They can't touch us in here.'

'Excellent work, everyone,' Drake said. He turned to Furan, who was standing beside him. 'Begin the retrieval operation.' Furan nodded and walked quickly off the bridge.

☢ ☢ ☢

On board Air Force One there were scenes of complete chaos. Secret-service agents took up positions around the President's office, their weapons drawn, waiting for whoever had captured the plane to make their next move.

Agent Fred Miller had only been in charge of the President's protection detail for three months and he was determined that this President was not going to be the first to be kidnapped. He walked the length of the specially converted 747, checking on his men as they set up defensive positions around the President and his staff. They were armed with light sub-machine guns that contained special low-velocity rounds that were specifically designed not to penetrate the skin of the aircraft. The last thing they wanted to risk was an explosive decompression of the plane if a firefight broke out. The downside, of course, was that they were less effective against enemy agents wearing body armour, but that could not be helped.

As Miller reached the forward section of the aircraft, the number of agents increased dramatically, forming a heavily armed ring around the President's office and the cockpit. Miller headed for the cockpit first. The two agents flanking the door acknowledged him with a nod, one of them tapping on the door. Inside, Colonel Woods heard the soft knock and checked the screen displaying a feed from the camera outside. He unlatched the armoured door and let Agent Miller on to the flight deck.

'What the hell is that thing?' Miller asked as he ducked down to get the best possible view of the underside of the Dreadnought's hull through the cockpit window.

'I have no idea,' Woods replied. 'I'm trained to recognise anything that flies and I've never seen anything like it.'

'It must be the size of an aircraft carrier,' Miller said, craning his neck to see if he could make out any more details of the giant aircraft. 'Chinese?'

'If it is then the CIA need to up their game,' Woods replied. 'Don't you think they would have an idea that they were building something like that?'

'Yeah,' Miller said, slightly distracted. 'What systems do you guys still have?'

'Nothing really, beyond basic support systems – lights, heat, air, that kind of thing. We're not going anywhere. We're moving at cruising speed, but even if we could get free we'd just drop like a stone without flight control systems.'

'I was afraid you were going to say that,' Miller replied. 'Keep trying to raise someone on comms. Whatever you do, don't let anyone in here.'

'Wasn't planning to,' Woods replied with a grim smile.

Miller nodded and headed back towards the President's office, where the majority of his men were positioned. He had a dozen men spread out in tactical positions around the office, all of whom were prepared to give their lives to protect the man inside. Miller knocked on the office door and a voice called out for him to enter. Miller stepped inside and nodded to the President and his Chief of Staff.

A military aide stood in one corner of the room, a black briefcase chained to his wrist.

'Mr President,' Miller said with a nod.

'Agent Miller,' the President replied, 'I was just explaining to Mike here that we are entirely in your hands at this point.'

'We won't let you down, sir,' Miller replied.

'Any idea of who did this yet?' the Chief of Staff asked.

'No, sir,' Miller replied honestly, 'though the resources required to carry out an operation of this nature would suggest that whoever's behind it is extremely well funded and organised.'

'Given that they've literally just plucked Air Force One out of the sky, I think that much is clear, Fred,' the President said, raising an eyebrow. 'Did any of the crew of the escort jets make it?'

'No, sir,' Miller replied, 'there were no chutes. They hit

us too hard and too fast.'

'And we have no communications, correct?' the President asked.

'No, sir. At this point I would normally recommend the use of the escape pod, but even that cannot be launched until we get control of our systems again,' Miller explained. Air Force One was equipped with a one-man escape pod, but whoever had taken control of the plane had locked down its launch controls along with all of the other major systems.

'Then we have little choice but to wait and see what our mysterious captors' next move is,' the President said with admirable calmness.

'I'm afraid it rather looks that way, sir.'

'I know that you and your men won't let us down,' the President added.

'Count on it, sir,' Miller replied and walked out of the office. He couldn't help but respect the President's ability to keep a cool head in a crisis like this. At least their attackers wanted them alive. If their intention had been to kill them, then they would have already done just that, and much as he hated to admit it, Miller knew that there wouldn't have been a damn thing that he could have done about it. He was just glad that the First Lady and the President's children had not been on board.

He went from man to man checking on his team. They

were the best of the best, chosen from the elite units of the armed forces and law enforcement for their unique skills and resolve. If they couldn't protect their commander-in-chief then no one could. He walked up to one of the newest recruits to the team, a graduate of the FBI's elite Hostage Rescue Team.

'Ready, Agent Jackson?' Miller asked.

'Born ready, s-irrr . . .' Jackson replied, slurring his words, his eyes losing focus. He looked at Miller for a moment, confused, and then his knees gave way and he collapsed to the floor. Miller tried to catch him but he too was feeling weak and disorientated. A little bit of his brain that was still functioning clearly fought to make his voice work properly.

'Gas!' Miller barked, flailing around for anything to grab on to. Whatever it was, it was colourless, odourless, fast-acting and filling every bit of the plane. He tried to take a step towards the locker where they kept the gas masks, but his legs wouldn't cooperate. He was the last of his men to drop unconscious to the ground.

On the lower deck the main hatch unlocked with a clunk and the door opened outwards. Furan led his men on to the plane, his pistol raised. He was not expecting to meet any resistance but he was not going to take any chances at this point. The gas that they had fed into the ventilation system had done its job; there appeared to be no one left conscious on board. Furan signalled for two of his men to follow him up the stairs to the upper deck and for the rest to deploy along the length of the plane. He pushed the unconscious secret-service agent slumped across the top of the stairs out of the way and moved quickly to the President's office.

As he opened the door he immediately spotted one of his targets. He did not look much like the most powerful man on the planet right now, lying unconscious on the floor next to his Chief of Staff. Furan signalled for the two men with him to take the President, then moved over to the corner of the room. He pulled a small aerosol from his belt and sprayed the liquid nitrogen inside on to the chain securing the briefcase to the military aide's wrist. Furan pulled at the case and the chain shattered like it was made of glass. He hurried out of the office and back to the main hatch, walking quickly back to the Dreadnought's external air-lock. Once inside he pulled off his gas mask and spoke quickly into his throat mic.

'Furan to control, we have the targets.'

☢ ☢ ☢

Raven pushed the unconscious engineer into the locker. He had, perhaps unsurprisingly under the circumstances, been all too keen to tell her exactly where to find Darkdoom, or at least the location of the Dreadnought's

240

brig, which was where he assumed they were being held. She had rewarded him for his cooperation by depriving him of consciousness rather than life.

Moving quickly through the engineering deck, she passed a thick plexiglass window which looked in on what she assumed must be the Dreadnought's fusion core. It was a huge, steel ring-shaped device that crackled with bright blue lightning and emitted a deep thrumming hum that she could feel as much as hear. Raven continued down the corridor to the staircase that would lead her to the upper decks. There were surprisingly few crew for a vessel of this size. She could only assume that Drake's experience in designing unmanned aerial vehicles had meant that many of the Dreadnought's systems were designed to function without human intervention.

As she reached the top of the staircase she heard voices nearby, heading in her direction. Raven leapt straight upwards and grabbed the exposed pipework that ran along the ceiling, pulling herself up into the shadows. She waited as a dozen well-armed men walked past beneath, oblivious to her presence. She weighed up her odds but she knew that even for her that was too many to take on at once. Then, just behind the heavily armed squad, Furan appeared carrying a black briefcase and walking along beside an unconscious figure on a stretcher. Raven could hardly believe her eyes as she recognised the man on the gurney – the face, the stars-and-stripes lapel pin, the immaculate dark blue suit. It made no sense, in fact it seemed impossible, but she couldn't deny the evidence of her own eyes. What on earth was Drake doing?

☣ ☣ ☣

Darkdoom stood in silence, watching the events unfold on the bridge. He knew Drake had been planning something spectacular and horrifying but he had not honestly expected anything on this scale. There was a reason that G.L.O.V.E. had always avoided operations of this nature in the past. Nation states were prepared to accept financial or material losses, but it was quite another matter when one directly attacked a head of state. In his experience it was akin to the difference between carefully opening a beehive and extracting the honey or, on the other hand, hitting the same beehive with a stick. One produced tangible rewards, the other a swarm of angry bees. The Americans especially. Attacking their President would bring their military and security forces down on the guilty parties like the wrath of God. Suddenly he began to understand why Drake appeared so keen for G.L.O.V.E. to be the fall guys for this operation.

'Ahhh, our celebrity guest has arrived,' Drake said happily as Furan's squad marched on to the bridge with their prize. Drake walked over to the stretcher and looked down at the unconscious figure lying on it.

'He's taller than I expected,' Drake said with a grin.

'We have what we need,' Furan said, 'Should we dispose of the other passengers from the plane?'

'No, not yet,' Drake replied. 'One can never have too many hostages. We'll get rid of them later when the operation's complete.' Drake gestured for a man in a white coat standing nearby to come forward. 'Wake him up.'

The man bent over the trolley and rolled up the President's sleeve before taking out a syringe and sliding the needle into his arm. After a few seconds his eyelids fluttered and then opened, a look of confusion was quickly replaced by one of anger.

'Hello Mr President,' Drake said with a smile, 'allow me to introduce myself.'

'I know who you are, Mr Drake,' the President replied. 'What I don't know is what exactly you hope to achieve with all this. This isn't just a kidnapping. A man as wealthy as you can't possibly want something as simple as money. If you were going to kill me, you'd have done it already. So what is it that you want?'

'Oh, I'm not going to kill you, Mr President,' Drake replied calmly, 'not yet anyway. There are a couple of things I need from you first.'

Drake gestured to the guards on either side of the President and they grabbed him roughly by the arms, restraining him. Drake stepped forwards and removed the President's tie and undid the top two buttons of his shirt. He reached inside and pulled a key on a chain from the President's neck. Furan stepped forward with the briefcase, placing it on the top of a nearby console. Drake turned the key in its lock, popping the latches open. As he opened the case there was a whirring sound and a small metal eyepiece rose up from the machine inside. Drake took out the plastic-coated folder that was packed into the case alongside the strange device.

'I can't kill you yet because there's one problem with retinal scanners, and that is that they don't work on a dead man's eye.'

He gestured again to the guards holding the President and they pushed him roughly towards the open briefcase. They forced the struggling President's head towards the eyepiece as he closed his eyes tightly.

'That's really quite pointless,' Drake said with a sigh. 'I could just cut your eyelid off but that would be so messy now, wouldn't it?' Drake grabbed his jaw and carefully forced the President's eyelid open. There was a flash from the eyepiece and the steel plate at the bottom of the case slid aside and a small keyboard rose up out of the hidden recess. One of Drake's technicians hurried forward as Drake offered him the plastic folder. The technician opened the folder and carefully typed in the series of coded entries that he found inside.

'We have access,' the technician said, swallowing nervously. 'Slaving system control to our terminals.'

'You know, I've never understood why they call this thing "the football",' Drake said, gesturing to the open case. 'I mean, it looks nothing like a football.'

Darkdoom took a long deep breath, trying to stay calm. Drake's words confirmed his worst fears. 'The football' was slang for the device that controlled access to the launch codes for America's entire nuclear arsenal and it now appeared to be under Drake's control. A truly terrifying prospect.

'This will never work, you know,' the President said defiantly. 'The moment that Air Force One went missing they will have instituted a protocol to physically prevent any missiles from launching until they know what has happened to me. You can't launch anything.'

'Silly me,' Drake said sarcastically. 'Why didn't I think of that? You're right, of course, but there is one critical exception. There's one launch platform they can't get to and physically deactivate and it's the only one I need. Tell me, Mr President, have you heard of Thor's Hammer?'

The President said nothing, but the way that his jaw muscles clenched as Drake mentioned the name suggested that he knew exactly what he was talking about.

'A fascinating device,' Drake continued, 'above top

secret, the blackest of black-budget projects. It took all of my resources to find out what it could do. Now what was it that my informant called it? . . . Oh yes, that's right, a "mountain cracker" – a nuclear missile fired from orbit that can pierce so far into the ground before detonating that it could destroy, for example, an entire underground terrorist base in the blink of an eye. Most impressive. And when combined with the tracking capabilities of my Overwatch satellites, it was originally intended to bring a quick and brutal end to the "War on Terror". Your prede-cessor nearly used it on several occasions, but there's still a certain negative press attached to the nuclear option. Just look at how people have reacted over the past few hours to me setting off one little nuclear bomb in the middle of the desert. Imagine the reaction if you were ever to use the thing against a target on foreign soil. So, despite the expense of developing it, it was looking as though it was destined to become just another military white elephant floating around in orbit. Until now that is.'

'Initiating manoeuvring thrusters,' the technician reported from the console that was now attached to the device in the briefcase. 'Time until target: forty-three minutes.'

'You see, I have a new target for Thor's Hammer,' Drake said with an evil grin. 'Not some mountain range on the other side of the planet; something much closer to home.'

He gestured at the screen behind them, where a digital map displayed a red cross hair moving towards an array of green target circles clustered in the north-western quarter of the United States.

'Have you ever been to Yellowstone national park, Mr President?' Drake asked. 'I'm told that it's quite beautiful. But not for very much longer, I'm afraid. Because once the missiles from Thor's Hammer hit at these locations,' he pointed at the map, 'it's going to cause a chain reaction that will trigger the supervolcano that lies beneath it. When that happens, you're going to be the President of the largest disaster zone in human history. Three quarters of the United States will be covered in a blanket of ash that will make human existence impossible. America will simply cease to exist as a world power and in the catastrophic global environmental and financial chaos that ensues it will be left to people of genuine vision, like myself, to pick up the pieces and create a new world order, a world without the malignant influence of your country, a world that we can shape in any image we choose.'

'You're insane,' the President said quietly, a look of shocked disbelief on his face.

'"In all matters of opinion, our adversaries are insane",' Drake said calmly, 'to quote Oscar Wilde. I think I'll keep you alive long enough to witness the results of my supposed insanity for yourself.'

Drake walked over to Darkdoom.

'You see, Diabolus, this is what G.L.O.V.E. has lost. If only Number One could have lived to see this.'

'Number One was psychotic,' Darkdoom growled, 'and so are you.'

'Oh, but that's the real beauty of this,' Drake said with an evil smile. 'Has it sunk in properly yet? It won't be me that the world remembers as the villain behind all this. Thanks to your little pre-recorded address it will be you and G.L.O.V.E. that take the blame. You're the one who will go down in history as the butcher of billions. They'll find your body in some suitably public place, an apparent suicide, presumably overwhelmed by the guilt of what you had done. I, on the other hand, will be remembered as one of the heroes who rebuilt the world.' He gestured to the guards flanking Darkdoom. 'Take him away.'

☹ ☹ ☹

Nero walked through the Shroud's cargo compartment, lost in thought. He struggled to hide his frustration at the fact that they had not been able to follow Drake.

'Doctor Nero, I think I've found something,' the Professor called to him from the other end of the bay, where he was still working on his laptop.

'What do you have, Professor?' Nero asked, walking towards him.

'There,' Professor Pike said, pointing at the screen. His laptop showed an image of the Atlantic Ocean that had been intercepted from a civilian weather satellite. In the centre of the image was a swirling mass of cloud.

'Now look at the image from sixty seconds before that,' the Professor said, tapping at the keyboard. The storm cell vanished. 'I'm no meteorologist, but as far as I know it's impossible for a natural storm to develop that quickly, even in the middle of the ocean.'

'The Dreadnought,' Nero said, carefully examining the two images.

'I think that's an entirely reasonable conclusion, yes,' the Professor replied. 'I've already taken the liberty of ordering the pilot to head to these coordinates. We should be at this location in about forty-five minutes.'

'So what's Drake up to in there and, more to the point, how do we get to him?' Nero asked.

'Just because any sane pilot would not choose to fly into a storm like that under normal circumstances doesn't mean that it can't be done,' the Professor replied. 'I won't lie to you though: it will not be a pleasant ride. I can't guarantee that we will make it through.'

'Very well,' Nero said after a few seconds. 'Order the other Shroud to return to H.I.V.E. There's no point risking both aircraft. I'll go and talk to the pilot.'

☻☻☻

Wing pushed Otto back against the wall as four guards walked past the end of the corridor, surrounding Diabolus Darkdoom, whose hands were cuffed in front of him.

'I think we may want to follow them,' Otto said.

Wing nodded. They shadowed the guards and their prisoner as discreetly as they could, and after a couple of minutes arrived at the Dreadnought's brig. The lead soldier from Darkdoom's escort walked up to the guard standing outside an armoured door.

'Drake wants him locked up again,' the soldier said. 'Open it up.'

The soldier turned back to the escort surrounding Darkdoom and was about to speak when he felt an arm slipping around his throat and the pistol being pulled from the holster on his belt. The last thing he heard as he lost consciousness was three gunshots.

Darkdoom looked down in astonishment at the three bodies that lay on the floor around him. The brig guard tossed the still-smoking pistol to the ground and stepped towards him, pulling off the black face mask and tactical goggles.

'Sorry I couldn't get here sooner,' Raven said, crouching down to search the body of one of the fallen guards.

'A pleasure to see you as always, Natalya,' Darkdoom said with a smile. 'Are you here alone?'

'Yes,' Raven said, her eyes widening in surprise as she

saw the two figures walking down the corridor behind Darkdoom. 'At least I thought I was.'

'If I'd known it was going to be a family reunion I'd have worn something smarter,' Otto said with a grin.

'Mr Malpense, Mr Fanchu,' Raven said, shaking her head slightly as she used the keys she had found on the fallen soldier to release Darkdoom's cuffs. 'I honestly wish I could say that it was a surprise to see you here, but let's face it . . .'

'I, for one, am glad to see all of you,' Darkdoom said, rubbing his wrists. He walked to the brig door and unbolted it. 'And I think I know someone else who will be too.' He opened the door and Nigel stepped out into the corridor. His look of confusion was replaced by a broad smile as he saw Otto, Wing and his father.

'What on earth are you doing here?' Nigel asked as he walked over to Otto.

'It's a . . . erm . . . long story,' Otto said with a crooked smile. 'I'll tell you later.'

'Where are the others?' Nigel asked.

'Safe . . . I hope,' Otto said. Now was not the time to tell Nigel about the catastrophic destruction of Drake's base in Nevada.

Raven noticed that Wing seemed to be hanging back, a look of slight disapproval on his face.

'Is there something wrong?' she asked him quietly.

'Was this . . . necessary?' he said, gesturing at the bodies on the floor.

'Three men with assault rifles surrounding a friendly target is not a situation that leaves much time for subtlety,' Raven said with a frown. 'In our world the non-lethal response is not always an option, Mr Fanchu. It is a lesson that, in time, you too will learn. Trust me.'

Wing looked back at her, his expression unreadable.

'Pleased as I am to see all of you, we have an urgent matter to attend to,' Darkdoom said.

'I'm going to assume that it has something to do with the high-profile prisoner I saw Furan with earlier,' Raven said cryptically.

'High profile?' Otto asked.

'You don't get much higher,' Darkdoom said and proceeded to explain the details of the plan that Drake had set in motion. 'I think it probably goes without saying that we have to stop this.' He looked at the shocked faces around him.

'Of course,' Raven replied, 'but how?'

'I might be able to do it,' Otto said, 'but I have to get on to the bridge.'

'Furan's men are going to be guarding it and once they realise what's just happened down here, which won't take long, they're going to be on a heightened state of alert,' Raven replied.

'Then we have to move quickly,' Darkdoom said, 'before Drake locks the Dreadnought down completely. Wing, you and Nigel should head to the hangar bay and see if you can procure us some transport. Raven, you take Otto to the bridge. I'll provide a diversion that should draw away most of the guards. Once I do, you need to stop those missiles from launching by whatever means necessary. Any questions?' he asked, looking at each of them in turn. 'No? Good. Let's go.'

☢ ☢ ☢

Nero looked out through the Shroud's cockpit window at the boiling black clouds of the enormous storm cell towering above the ocean, the vast formations lit from within by flashes of lightning.

'You're sure about this?' the pilot asked nervously.

'Absolutely,' Nero replied, 'we have to get inside.'

'OK. You'd better get below and make sure everyone's strapped in. This isn't going to be a smooth ride,' the pilot said, reaching up and flicking a couple of switches on a control panel on the ceiling.

Nero climbed down the ladder to the passenger compartment, where Francisco was hurriedly strapping down the loose equipment crates.

'We're nearly at the storm front, Colonel,' Nero said. 'Make sure everyone and everything's secure down here.'

'Yes, sir,' Francisco replied, pulling the cargo straps tight on a large metallic crate.

Nero moved through the Shroud, past the H.I.V.E. security team operatives who filled the crowded compartment, to where his four recently rescued students were buckling up the harnesses attached to their seats.

'Mr Argentblum, ladies,' Nero said, 'I'm sorry that we couldn't return directly to H.I.V.E. but there is one more thing we have to do. We do not leave our people behind, I'm sure you can appreciate that.'

'Of course,' Laura said, speaking for them all.

'Good,' Nero said. 'We're going to be experiencing some . . . turbulence.'

'I am not liking the sound of that,' Franz said nervously as Nero walked back towards the cockpit ladder. 'I am not liking the sound of that at all.'

chapter twelve

Otto waited as Raven retrieved her twin swords from their hiding place amid the pipes that ran along the ceiling and strapped them to her back. She had kept the body armour that she'd 'borrowed' from the man guarding the brig, as well as one of the assault rifles from the fallen men who had been escorting Darkdoom. She looked very much like someone with whom you did not want to mess.

'Right, once Diabolus has drawn off the guards we're going to hit the bridge hard and fast,' Raven explained. 'If anyone starts shooting, keep your head down. All of this will have been for nothing if you catch a bullet. Understood?'

Otto nodded and the pair of them set off, keeping a careful look out for Drake's men. When they reached a junction with the corridor leading to the bridge, Raven carefully peeked around the corner. She raised her hand, indicating with four fingers. How many guards she could see. There were bound to be more inside.

The pair of them waited in the shadows, not knowing how long it would take for Darkdoom to provide the necessary diversion. A couple of interminable minutes passed and Otto was just starting to convince himself that something had gone wrong when the alarms sounded. Raven pushed him back out of sight behind a storage locker as Furan and the guards from outside the bridge ran down the corridor, heading for the stairs that led to the lower decks.

They waited a few more seconds and then approached the bridge door. Raven hit the switch next to the door as Otto took cover to one side. It slid open with a hiss and she burst into the room, scanning for any immediate threats. The bridge crew were sat at their stations, leaving only two guards flanking the President. Drake turned as she entered and Raven felt a grim satisfaction at the horri-fied shock in his eyes as she levelled her rifle at him.

'Nobody move,' Raven shouted to the bridge crew and the two remaining guards. 'Anyone so much as looks at me funny and Drake's the first to die, understood?'

The guards on either side of the President tensed, as if considering their options, but quickly realised that she had the drop on them.

'You two,' she shouted at the guards, 'pop the magazines and then put the rifles on the ground. Slowly.'

The men did as they were told and then raised their hands.

'Otto, get in here!' Raven yelled, keeping the gun trained on Drake.

'You really are very irritating, you know,' Drake said. 'I should have had Furan kill you in New York. I won't make the same mistake again.'

'You won't get another chance,' Raven growled.

Otto hurried on to the bridge and quickly spotted the black briefcase that was connected to the weapon control terminal. He unplugged the cable connecting it to the console and closed the case.

'That won't do any good,' Drake said smugly. 'The orders have been issued. You can't countermand them without access to the satellite communications grid, and only I have the code.'

'Give it to me,' Raven said, stepping forward and pressing the muzzle of the rifle to Drake's forehead.

'No,' Drake replied, 'I don't think I will. In fact I think you'll give me that rifle and put your hands in the air.'

Raven felt something cold and hard press into the back of her skull.

'Sloppy, Natalya,' Furan said, cocking the hammer on the pistol he held to her head. 'Poorly planned and poorly executed. I thought I'd trained you better than that.'

Raven lowered the rifle and let it fall to the deck.

'Mr Malpense, I presume,' Drake said with a smile as he walked towards Otto. 'Now, if you don't mind, I'll take that.' He held out his hand for the briefcase and Otto reluctantly give it to him. 'I assume since you two are here that it's Darkdoom running around causing trouble down in engineering. Not to worry. My men will find him soon enough.'

He stared at Otto for a moment.

'I've been doing some research on you, Mr Malpense, or may I call you Otto?' Drake said. 'Some friends of mine provided me with quite a detailed file on you and your special abilities after you started to make a nuisance of yourself. I'm curious. What's it like to be able to do what you can do? I'd imagine it must be quite a unique sensation. I have to say I was really quite impressed with the way you bypassed the security on the servers at my building in New York. I designed the security system myself. It was supposed to be quite impregnable and yet you got around it in just a couple of minutes. You know, you don't have to die with Darkdoom and the rest of the idiots that follow him. There could be a place for you in our new world. You could be a valuable asset. What do you think?'

'I think you're a nut job with a god complex that likes the sound of his own voice just a little too much,' Otto said with a nasty smile.

Drake gave a single short laugh and then backhanded Otto hard across the face, knocking him to his knees. Otto tasted blood in his mouth as he stood back up, a look of defiance on his face.

'I see Nero already has his hooks too far into you for you to be of any further use to me. Such a shame,' Drake said, turning away. He stopped for a moment and then turned back towards Otto. 'Tell me one thing though, Mr Malpense. Why haven't you just taken control of the Dreadnought? Surely, given what you can do, you could just have infiltrated her control systems. They are well secured, admittedly, but no more so than the systems in New York. It would certainly have been more effective than this –' he gestured at Raven – 'brute force approach.'

'You know perfectly well why I didn't,' Otto replied. 'I couldn't. But I suppose that's why you integrated that black filth into your network.'

'Black . . . What on earth are you talking about?' Drake asked, looking genuinely confused.

'The organic supercomputer,' Otto said, 'the black slime that you've got running through your system.'

'Just how stupid do you think I am, Mr Malpense,' Drake replied impatiently. 'Firstly, there's no such thing as an organic supercomputer, not yet anyway, and secondly, I would certainly never integrate something like that with the Dreadnought's systems, even if it did exist.'

'You really don't know, do you?' Otto said quietly.

'Know what?' Drake demanded angrily.

'Why don't you just take a look for yourself?' Otto suggested, nodding towards a cabling access panel on a nearby wall.

Drake stared at him for a moment and then moved over to the panel, unclipping it and removing it from the wall. There, clearly visible, intertwined with the other cabling, was a seething mass of glistening black tendrils. They seemed almost to pulse, as if in time with the data that coursed through the other wires. Drake looked at them with a mixture of confusion and revulsion.

'What is this?' he said, sounding genuinely bewildered. 'Who put this into my ship?'

'I did,' Furan said, pushing Raven towards Otto and Drake, covering them all with his pistol.

☹ ☹ ☹

The Shroud lurched violently to the left, its engines screaming in protest as the full force of nature's fury tried to swat it from the sky. The pilot fought with the controls, a thin film of sweat covering his pale face. 'I'm not sure how much more of this we can take,' he shouted over the noise of the labouring engines and the howling of the storm outside.

Suddenly there was a bright white flash and an

enormous cracking sound as the Shroud was struck by a bolt of lightning. The engines stuttered for a moment and then roared back into life. A series of flashing red warning lights lit up across the control panel in front of the pilot.

'We've lost cloaking,' the pilot said, an edge of panic in his voice.

Nero was sitting strapped into the seat behind the pilot and he could understand why the man was concerned. Without cloaking engaged there was nothing to stop the Dreadnought spotting them the moment they left the storm clouds. That was, of course, assuming that they made it through the storm in the first place.

Down in the passenger compartment the situation was no better. Francisco's men were hardened soldiers, men who were used to putting their lives on the line, but even so he could almost smell the fear in the air. They were in the hands of Mother Nature now and she was not happy.

'We are all going to be dying, we are all going to be dying,' Franz whimpered at the other end of the compartment. 'I don't want to die, especially not on an empty stomach. Oooooh God!'

Lucy leant over and whispered in his ear. '*Sleep.*'

Franz looked surprised for a moment and then his chin dropped on to his chest as he fell unconscious.

'On behalf of everyone, thank you,' Shelby said, her

knuckles white where she clung on to her seat harness.

'My pleasure,' Lucy said through gritted teeth as the Shroud plunged downwards again before slowly clawing its way back to higher altitude.

'You couldn't do the same thing for me, could you?' Laura asked, only half joking.

Back on the flight deck, Nero winced as another bolt of lightning struck the Shroud. The pilot growled as he pulled hard on the joystick, almost willing the ailing aircraft to stay airborne. Then just as suddenly as their roller-coaster ride had started, it stopped, and the Shroud punched out through the interior wall of the storm cell and into the area of calm surrounding the Dreadnought.

'Good God, is that what I think it is?' the pilot said as they both saw the plane suspended by giant clamps under the belly of the Dreadnought with its unmistakable blue and white livery.

'I'm afraid it is,' Nero said quietly. 'What has Drake done?'

☺ ☺ ☺

Down on the engineering deck of the Dreadnought, Darkdoom knew he was running out of time. He scanned the control panel in front of him, trying to work out the best way to disable the safety interlocks on the system without alerting anyone on the bridge. He was relatively

262

familiar with the ship's systems, but this was still beyond his experience.

'You don't need to know how something works in order to break it, Diabolus,' he whispered to himself. He flicked a couple of switches and twisted a large black handle that was underneath a screen displaying a series of green bars. As he twisted the handle the bars began to get longer, first turning yellow, then orange and finally red. 'Well, that looks promising,' he said with a slight smile.

He pulled the pistol he had taken from one of the fallen guards in the brig and pointed it at the control panel, emptying the clip into the machine. Nobody was going to be undoing his sabotage any time soon. He heard voices coming from the other end of the compartment. That was hardly surprising given that he'd made a point of setting off as many intruder alarms as he could on his way through the engineering deck. He just hoped that he'd provided enough of a diversion for Raven and Otto in the process. It was time to go.

☣ ☣ ☣

'What do you mean, *you* did this?' Drake said, staring in amazement at Furan.

'It was not difficult,' Furan replied calmly. 'The substance is self-replicating. I only needed to insert a tiny amount into the system while the Dreadnought was docked in Nevada; it was already programmed to do the rest. The Disciples call it Animus – I do not begin to understand how it works, I just know that it is some kind of organic computer that takes control of any system it's inserted into.'

'I don't understand,' Drake said. 'Why would you do this?'

'Because our esteemed guest over there was right,' Furan said, gesturing towards the President. 'You *are* insane. I've always known it and so have the rest of the Disciples, but until now we needed you. We needed your technology, your contacts in the military, your ship, but we knew that once those missiles detonated and the world was ours for the taking that you would be too much of a loose cannon to keep around. We knew that we were going to have to dispose of you and this ship. But how could we be sure that we could take control of its systems, that you wouldn't have locked us out? Fortunately, technology that we have recently developed made that quite simple. As soon as the Dreadnought launched, the substance you just found began to multiply and integrate seamlessly into your systems, allowing us to seize control when the right time came. I'm afraid Mr Malpense has rather spoilt the surprise but, no matter. It just means that you learn that you are surplus to requirements a little ahead of schedule.'

'Surplus to requirements?' Drake yelled. 'This was my plan. Without me there would be nothing, and this is how the Disciples repay me?'

'You've served your purpose and so has the Dreadnought. We cannot take the chance that at some point in the future you might turn against us, or worse, reveal our part in the catastrophe that is about to befall the United States. You're a dangerous loose end, one that it is now my job to cut off. Goodbye Jason.'

Furan fired twice, both rounds hitting Drake squarely in the chest and he dropped to his knees, eyes wide, before slowly toppling forward and hitting the deck with a thud. There were a couple of angry cries from members of the bridge crew but these were quickly silenced by the arrival of more of Furan's men. They raised their rifles and kept Drake's people covered. Furan looked at his watch.

'Ten minutes to impact,' he said and turned to one of his men. 'Take the President back to Air Force One and take this with you.' He handed the man the black brief-case that was the key to America's nuclear arsenal. 'They both need to be on board so that no questions are raised if and when the wreckage is retrieved.'

The soldier nodded and he and one of his comrades forced the President towards the door at gunpoint. Furan gestured to two more of his men.

'You and you, get rid of that,' he said, pointing at

Drake's body. 'Now, what to do with you two.' He smiled evilly at Otto and Raven. 'It seems such a waste to just kill you. I know for a fact that at least one other senior member of the Disciples would very much like to dissect you, Mr Malpense, and Raven, you have always been my greatest unfinished project. The truth is, though, that you are both too dangerous to leave alive, too loyal to our enemies, too difficult to turn. So I'm afraid it's goodbye Mr Malpense, dosvidaniya Natalya.' He raised his pistol.

Outside the bridge windows something suddenly lit up with an impossibly white light. The Zeus Sphere reached its limits as the terminal overcharge that Darkdoom had accidentally set in motion reached its climax and the giant ball at the prow of the Dreadnought detonated catastrophically. The bridge windows blew out in a lethal hail of flying glass and the pressurised air raced out through the gaping holes. Several of the bridge crew and a couple of Furan's men were sucked out of the windows, their screams vanishing in the roaring wind. Furan was blown off his feet, his pistol scattering away across the floor as he grabbed desperately for something to hang on to. Heavy steel emergency shutters slammed down, sealing the bridge windows as the pressure loss was detected and the bridge was plunged into darkness for a few seconds before emergency lighting came online, illuminating the chaotic scene with a dim red light. Furan struggled to stand, blood trickling into his eye from a vicious gash on his forehead. Raven and the boy were nowhere to be seen.

☣ ☣ ☣

Wing felt the deck move as an enormous shudder ran through the Dreadnought's hull, accompanied by the muffled sound of an explosion.

'What was that?' Nigel said as the whole ship seemed to emit a low-pitched groan.

'Nothing good, I suspect,' Wing replied with a frown. 'But we may have a bigger problem.' He looked out across the hangar deck. There was only a single Shroud in the whole bay and it was surrounded by at least a dozen of Furan's men. He and Nigel were concealed behind a large fuel tank fifty or sixty metres away at the other end of the hangar.

'Now what do we do?' Nigel asked, pushing his glasses back up on to the bridge of his nose.

'Honestly, I have no idea,' Wing said. He had been trained well enough by the tutors at H.I.V.E. to be able to recognise a tactically hopeless situation when he saw one, and this was exactly that.

Suddenly there was the sound of another distant explosion and this time the whole deck seemed to tip violently towards the starboard side of the ship. Wing struggled to keep his footing, grabbing on to Nigel and stopping him from sliding away across the deck. The docking clamps holding the Shroud to the hangar floor groaned in protest and a few of the soldiers surrounding it fell to the ground.

'I think we need to find a way off this ship sooner rather than later,' Darkdoom said from behind them.

'What's going on, Dad?' Nigel asked.

'My attempts at diversionary sabotage may have been a little . . . overenthusiastic,' Darkdoom replied, sounding slightly embarrassed.

There was the sound of another explosion from some-where off in the distance.

'I think we *really* need to get off this ship,' Nigel said uneasily.

☻ ☻ ☻

Otto and Raven ran down the corridor towards the hangar bay. They rounded a corner and Raven suddenly stopped. At the far end of the corridor were the President and the guards from the bridge who were escorting him back to Air Force One. They turned into a doorway at the end of corridor and disappeared from view.

'I can stop this,' Otto said.

'What do you mean?' Raven asked, looking back down the corridor they had just come down for any signs of pursuit.

'If I can get that briefcase, then I think I can stop the

268

satellite from launching its missiles,' Otto replied.

'You heard what Furan said about "the wreckage",' Raven said with a frown. 'They're planning to crash that plane.'

'I'm not stupid,' Otto replied quickly. 'I know that there's no way to save the people on board but we could be talking about hundreds of millions of people dying if Yellowstone blows, not to mention global environmental chaos and financial meltdown, the blame for all of which will be placed squarely on G.L.O.V.E.'s shoulders. I can't just stand by and let it happen. I have to at least try to stop it.'

Raven looked Otto square in the eye. She may have had a lot of blood on her own hands but she knew what he meant. If Drake's plan worked it would mean indiscriminate slaughter on an unprecedented scale. Not only that, it would mean the end of G.L.O.V.E. Anyone who had ever had anything to do with the organisation would be hunted to the ends of the earth if Drake's plan to pin the blame on them worked.

'I'll come with you,' Raven said.

'No,' Otto replied, 'they need you in the hangar bay. Don't worry, I have no intention of tangling with any of Furan's men. I leave that kind of thing to you and Wing. As soon as I'm done I'll head for the hangar. I'll be right behind you. This won't take long.'

Raven hesitated for a moment, weighing up the risks.

'Make it quick,' she said, 'and good luck.'

'Let's hope I don't need it,' Otto said with a tiny smile.

Raven gave him a small nod and Otto quickly headed after the President. He opened the Dreadnought's external airlock and crept down the stairs to the forward door of Air Force One, listening for any signs of Furan's men. As he stepped inside the plane he could hear voices coming from the stairs leading to the upper deck.

'OK, get to the hangar,' a gruff voice said. 'Furan's ordered a full evacuation.'

Otto ducked into the galley opposite the door and hid behind a bulkhead as the men filed quickly off the plane, resealing the door behind them. Otto waited a moment before coming out from his hiding place and heading to the upper deck. Unconscious bodies lay everywhere, everyone from flight attendants to bulky men in dark suits, some of whom were still holding the weapons they'd been wielding when they fell. He hurried up the stairs, looking for any sign of the President. He noticed that a nearby door with the presidential seal on it was standing slightly ajar and he pushed it open cautiously.

'Hello?' a voice said from inside.

'Hi,' Otto said as he walked into the room. The President sat behind his desk, each hand cuffed to one arm of the chair. 'Where's the case?'

The President nodded towards a filing cabinet on the other side of the room. The case sat on top of it.

'Mr Malpense, wasn't it?' the President asked. 'What exactly are you doing here?'

'Trying to stop this nightmare from happening,' Otto said, popping the latches on the case. 'And much as I'd like to discuss it, we really haven't got much time.'

Suddenly there was a clunking sound from somewhere overhead.

'That doesn't sound good,' Otto said quietly and then the floor seemed to drop away from beneath him.

☠ ☠ ☠

'Docking clamps disengaged,' one of Furan's men reported, looking up from the screen in front of him. 'Payload away.'

Furan had activated the direct wireless interface with the Animus that now coursed through the Dreadnought's hull giving him direct control of the giant vessel without the need for any of the recently deceased Drake's command codes.

'Sir, I have multiple radar contacts heading this way. Judging by their size and speed they have to be fighters,' another of his men reported.

'So the Americans have come to see what has happened to their President,' Furan said. 'What is their ETA?'

'Four minutes, sir,' the man at the tactical station replied. 'The storm cloak surrounding the Dreadnought has dissipated since the destruction of the Zeus Sphere and weapons systems are non-responsive, presumably due to the damage caused by the explosion. There's nothing to stop them blowing us out of the sky.'

'Very well, then it is time to leave,' Furan said. 'Transfer the primary control interface to my system on board the Shroud. Clear the bridge.'

His men quickly gathered their equipment and headed for the hangar bay. Furan looked at his watch again. There was now only three minutes until the missiles were launched from orbit and nothing could stop that now.

☹ ☹ ☹

Nero watched in astonishment as the giant blue and white plane detached from the underside of the Dreadnought and dropped away. The 747's nose began to point downwards, going into what would soon become an uncontrolled dive. There was nothing that anyone could do to save Air Force One now; its next stop would be the surface of the Atlantic Ocean, thirty thousand feet below.

'Head for the hangar,' Nero ordered the pilot. 'If any of our people are still alive on board that thing, that's where they'll be heading.'

'Sir, without our cloak the anti-aircraft weapons on the

272

Dreadnought are going to rip us to pieces,' the pilot said nervously.

'If those systems were active and functioning properly, I rather suspect we would already be a cloud of burning debris,' Nero said. 'I think whoever's currently in control of the Dreadnought has rather more pressing concerns at the moment.'

As if in response to Nero's words, a huge explosion ripped through one of the four clusters of engines that kept the giant aircraft aloft. Slowly, almost imperceptibly at first, the blazing tangle of wreckage at the front of the ship, where the storm-generating Zeus Sphere had once been, tipped downwards. The Dreadnought too was going down.

'The hangar. Now!' Nero snapped.

☺ ☺ ☺

Raven stuck her head around the corner of the large doorway that led on to the hangar bay. At the far end there were at least a dozen of Furan's men guarding a solitary Shroud. She looked around the bay for any signs of Darkdoom and the others. After a few seconds she spotted Darkdoom's head pop out from behind a fuel tank on the other side of the bay and then disappear again. There was another loud rumbling explosion from somewhere outside and the deck lurched sickeningly. Raven took advantage of the distraction to dash stealthily across to Darkdoom's hiding place while the guards struggled to stay on their feet. She found Diabolus, Nigel and Wing all crouched in the cramped space behind the bulky tank.

'You might want to be a bit more careful,' Raven said. 'You weren't exactly difficult to spot.'

'Fortunately, I think our friends over there are more concerned with getting themselves out of here than looking out for intruders,' Darkdoom said with a crooked smile. There was another muffled crump and the deck shook again. 'As you can see, my attempts at sabotage were rather overzealous.'

'Trust me, I'm not complaining,' Raven said quietly. 'You saved our skins, that's for sure.'

'Where's Otto?' Wing asked, looking concerned.

'He's on his way. There was something he had to take care of,' Raven replied. 'In the meantime we need to secure a way off this death trap.'

There were the sounds of more running feet from over by the entrance to the bay and Raven risked a quick look to see what was going on. Furan and another dozen of his men ran on to the hangar deck. Raven had been hoping that he might have been seriously injured during the chaos on the bridge a few minutes earlier, but it looked like he had escaped relatively unscathed.

'Where's Drake?' Darkdoom asked as he saw Furan too.

'Drake's dead,' Raven replied.

'I knew we could count on you, Natalya,' Darkdoom said with relief.

'It wasn't me, it was Furan,' Raven said and then quickly recounted the events on the bridge.

'Whoever these Disciples are, they certainly like to do a clean job,' Darkdoom said finally. 'Such ruthlessness is almost admirable.'

'Unfortunately Drake's plan did not die with him,' Raven said. 'They seem quite happy for that to proceed as scheduled.'

She watched as Furan hit the controls to seal the hangar access door and then aimed his pistol at the control panel.

'No!' Raven spat, moving to try and stop him, but she was too late. He fired three times into the panel and it disintegrated in a shower of sparks.

Furan heard her cry and spun around, aiming the pistol in her direction and snapping off a couple of shots without aiming. The bullets ricocheted harmlessly off the floor and the wall behind her as he turned and ran after his men, who were hurriedly boarding the Shroud.

Raven sprinted across the hangar bay as Furan ran up the loading ramp at the rear of the Shroud, which started to close behind him. He turned back towards Raven as she raced across the hangar towards him.

'Goodbye Natalya!' he yelled over the noise of the Shroud's engines. 'I'd say we'll meet again, but frankly that looks unlikely under the circumstances.' He gave her a quick wave as the ramp rose into place, sealing the Shroud's rear hatch.

The clamps securing the Shroud to the deck released and the dropship's idling engines roared into life as it began to lift off. Raven leapt into the air and slashed at one of the giant turbine engines, the crackling blade of her katana scything through the armoured casing. There was a loud bang and a cloud of black smoke belched out of the engine as Raven was knocked to the ground by the ailing thruster's downdraught. The hangar doors began to grind open and the air rushed out of the rapidly depressurising bay. Raven rammed her sword into the deck and clung on as the howling wind tried to drag her towards the widening gap between the hangar doors. After a few seconds the bay doors were far enough open and Furan's Shroud moved forward, straining for lift with just one functioning engine, and passed through the gap and out into the sky. Raven cursed loudly in Russian as the dropship's stealth systems engaged and it disappeared from view.

She immediately felt the bitter cold and lack of oxygen at this altitude, battling for breath as hypoxia began inevitably to set in. She struggled to her feet. Furan had escaped – there was nothing she could do about that now. She just needed to concentrate on getting the others off the Dreadnought. The only problem was that she had no idea how. She walked slowly over to where Darkdoom sat huddled with Nigel.

'Furan escaped,' Raven whispered hoarsely, the air almost too thin for speech. Darkdoom just nodded and then winced as the largest explosion yet tore through the ship and the deck slowly started to tip.

Suddenly there was a roar of engine noise from behind Raven and she turned to see a Shroud manoeuvring carefully into the hangar bay. She felt a flood of relief as the secondary loading ramp under the Shroud's nose descended to reveal Francisco standing in the hatchway, frantically waving at them.

'Go!' Raven barked at Darkdoom, who simply nodded and hurried with Nigel over to the waiting Shroud. Raven ran over to where Wing knelt, desperately pulling at the handle of the jammed hangar entrance door.

'We have to go now,' Raven croaked at Wing, fighting to fill her lungs with what little oxygen there was.

'I'm not leaving without Otto,' Wing said firmly.

There was an explosion somewhere on the other side of the door.

'Wing,' Raven said quietly, 'Otto's not coming.'

Wing punched the steel door, wanting with all his heart

to believe that she was wrong but knowing she was not. He nodded once and they both ran towards the Shroud, sprinting up the ramp as it closed. The dropship backed carefully out of the hangar and rotated in the air before its engines flared and it rocketed away from the doomed Dreadnought.

☙ ☙ ☙

'This is Wildcat to all wings,' the flight leader said into his mask, 'engage and destroy.' His orders were quite clear: he was to take out the giant aircraft before it crossed into United States airspace. He didn't know what it was or where it was from, but he was going to make damn sure it never made it that far.

'Joker Tally,' his wingman signalled, indicating that he was initiating his attack run.

Wildcat looked out over his starboard wing and Joker's F-22 banked hard towards the target.

'Fox two,' Joker signalled and a Sidewinder missile streaked out from the belly of his jet and speared into the threat aircraft's superstructure, detonating in a huge ball of fire. The flight leader watched as multiple other missile trails followed in its wake, turning the giant aircraft into a blazing wreck that began a terminal descent towards the Atlantic.

He was about to begin his own attack run when he

noticed something out of the corner of his eye.

'Sweet Jesus,' the flight leader whispered, shocked. 'Joker, form up on my wing now!' He banked his aircraft hard and sent it roaring in pursuit of the unmistakable shape of Air Force One as it plummeted towards the ocean below.

☣ ☣ ☣

Otto struggled to his feet as the giant plane's airframe shuddered. It was eerily quiet; there was no engine noise, but the fact that they were not nosediving towards the Atlantic meant that at least they had been released at a high enough speed to be in some sort of glide. He resisted the urge to calculate how long they had at this angle of descent before they hit the ocean. Unfortunately, he didn't have to do the maths to know that it wouldn't be long.

He ran out of the President's office and down the short aisle leading to the cockpit. He rattled the handle on the armoured door but it was firmly locked. He quickly tried to think of a way through the door but he knew it was pointless: cockpit doors were designed to withstand exactly that kind of improvised assault.

He ran back to the President's office as the plane shuddered again, more violently this time. He realised that the floor was already at a steeper angle than it had been just a few moments before.

'I need you to unlock this,' Otto said quickly, placing the opened case on the desk in front of the President and raising the retinal scanner into position.

'It won't do any good,' the President replied. 'It's reliant on the plane's communications array to transmit commands, and unless I'm way off the mark, we don't have any power.'

'Leave that to me,' Otto said and closed his eyes. The systems he felt all around him were dead. There was no power and without the engines running there was no way to generate any. He extended his senses, hunting for any trace of power, any electronic circuit that showed signs of life. There was the faintest glow in a far corner of the dead grid that surrounded him. He reached out for it: it was a simple switch powered by a battery. Without even really knowing what he was doing, he mentally threw the switch.

Underneath them, a ram air turbine popped out of the belly of the giant aircraft, the small fan spinning furiously in the high-speed air passing over the skin of the aircraft. The tiny machine produced just enough emergency power to activate some of the plane's critical systems and Otto sensed some of the dead electronic grid that surrounded him flaring into life. He reached for the communication system, checking that it had enough power for what he wanted it to do.

He opened his eyes briefly and looked at the President, who was looking at him like he'd gone crazy.

'I agree that now would be a good time for prayer,' the President said, 'but I was hoping you might be able to do something a little more tangible.'

'Oh, I'm not praying,' Otto said, 'but you can if you think it will help. What I really need you to do is to put your eye up to that thing.'

The President looked curiously at him for a moment before putting his eye to the scanner, which bleeped, and the access light inside the case turned green.

Otto closed his eyes again. Now he was going to have to do something that he had never done before, something that, if he was honest, he really didn't want to do at all. He immersed himself in the digital world once again, reaching out for the communications systems and connecting with them.

'OK mystery guest inside my head, if you're going to help me, now would be the time,' Otto whispered to himself.

For several long moments Otto felt nothing, and then a familiar voice whispered in his ear.

'We are stronger together than apart.'

Otto tensed as he felt the power of his abilities increase ten-fold. He sensed the data connections between the ailing aircraft and the ground and raced along them, feeling his consciousness expand geometrically as it coursed through the world's data networks. He felt like a god, his mind seeming to fill for an instant with the sum total of human knowledge, overwhelming him, burying him, erasing his personality.

'No,' Otto said, gritting his teeth and pulling back before he passed the point of no return. He focused the power he felt, reaching out for a ground-based transmission station in the right part of the globe and sending a handshake communication, searching for the right receiver.

'*There!*'

He brushed against the systems controlling Thor's Hammer, greeting the satellite with the right binary handshake before channelling the command codes from the briefcase next to him into its command core. The satellite immediately recognised his authority and cancelled the launch sequence. Only then did Otto allow himself to read the countdown to launch embedded within the system. There had been nine seconds left on the clock when he had countermanded the launch instructions.

Otto felt a searing pain in his head, as if something was swelling inside his skull. He wanted to pull back, to withdraw from the vast labyrinths of data, but there was still more to do. He took a deep breath and kept searching. Finding what he needed, he integrated himself seamlessly into the computer systems of the company he required, brushing aside their multiple layers of network security as if they were barely there at all. He searched out and downloaded the schematics and digital manuals that he wanted, absorbing them, learning their content as thoroughly as if he'd been studying them for years. Only then did he allow himself to return to his body. He slumped forwards on to the floor of the President's office, a thundering pain in his head and blood pouring from his nose. The President struggled against the cuffs securing him to his chair, wanting to assist Otto, but he was powerless to help.

'It's over,' Otto said, his voice broken and weak. 'I've aborted the launch.'

'What do you mean?' the President asked, sounding confused. 'How could you . . . ? I mean . . .'

'You'll just have to take my word for it,' Otto said through gritted teeth. He was exhausted. All he wanted was to sleep, for something, anything, to stop the constant stabbing pain in his head, but there was still one more thing he needed to do.

He closed his eyes again, focusing through the pain, and reached out using the knowledge he had just acquired to interface with the avionics system. He started the engines and began to pull the giant plane out of its terminal dive. He tried hard to ignore the numbers from the altimeter as Air Force One's nose slowly came up. The plane shook, the battered airframe groaning under the excessive loads that were being put on it. Their altitude dipped below a thousand feet just for a moment before Otto sensed that the nose was at the right angle and pushed the engines to their capacity and beyond, dragging the giant plane back into the sky and sending it climbing slowly up to a proper cruising altitude. Otto re-engaged the autopilot; he no longer had the strength or desire to even think about changing its destination. It would make little difference anyway: wherever this particular plane landed there would be a reception party waiting for them. Otto had a dim sense that this was probably not a good thing before he gave in to the pain in his head and lost consciousness.

chapter thirteen

'Where's Otto?' Laura asked as Wing sat down in the seat next to her.

'I . . . I do not know,' Wing said sadly, staring at the Shroud's floor.

'What do you mean?' Laura asked frantically. Wing just shook his head.

'Oh God . . . no,' Laura gasped, the reality of what Wing was saying slowly sinking in. She let out a sob as the tears came and Shelby hugged her.

'Come on,' Shelby said, fighting back tears herself, 'it's going to be all right.' But even as she said it she knew it wasn't true.

'What is being wrong?' Franz asked Nigel as his friend sat down next to him.

'Otto didn't make it,' Nigel said sadly.

'Oh . . .' Franz said, looking for a moment like he was going to say something but then thinking better of it.

Lucy sat and watched the reactions of her classmates, suddenly feeling very much like an outsider again. She'd heard all the talk about how dangerous life at H.I.V.E. was and had initially assumed it was just exaggeration, but now she was starting to realise that it was not.

Raven climbed the ladder to the flight deck and Nero got up, offering her the second seat behind the pilot, which she gratefully accepted.

'What happened?' Nero asked.

Raven quickly recounted the events on board the Dreadnought.

'So Otto was on board Air Force One when it was released?' Nero asked.

'I believe so, yes,' Raven replied, suddenly feeling very tired.

'Any sign of it on radar?' Nero asked.

'It disappeared from our radar about five minutes ago,' the pilot said, 'it was at two thousand feet and still dropping just before it went out of range.'

He did not need to tell them what that meant.

'Excuse me for a moment. There's one more thing to check,' Nero said. He climbed down the ladder to the lower deck and Raven let out a long sigh. A minute or so later he returned.

'You'll be glad to hear that Yellowstone national park appears still to be there,' Nero said. 'Professor Pike has just checked the very latest satellite imagery and there are no signs of any sort of thermonuclear detonation anywhere in the area.' He gave Raven a small, sad smile.

'He did it,' Raven said, closing her eyes, 'he damn well did it.'

☢ ☢ ☢

The men in the air-traffic control tower at Andrews Air Force Base watched nervously as the 747 touched down perfectly. They had been unable to make any sort of contact with Air Force One as it had come in to land. It had been shadowed by an entire squadron of F-22s as it had crossed into United States airspace. Any other aircraft would have been shot down long before it was allowed to land at an air force base with no ground-to-air contact having been made. The pilots of the fighters escorting the plane had reported no response from the flight crew and there was every reason to believe that she had to be landing on full automatic. Nobody had any idea what had happened since they'd lost contact with the President's plane, but the fact that it appeared to have been intercepted by an unknown hostile aircraft of a type no one had ever seen before suggested that something very bad might have happened. As the tyres touched the landing strip with only the tiniest puff of white smoke, emergency vehicles of every imaginable type raced on to the tarmac behind it, pursuing it in a speeding convoy of flashing lights.

The first vehicles to arrive as the plane rolled to a stop in the middle of the runway were a series of black trucks that formed a protective cordon around the plane. Men in body armour poured out of the rear doors as a mobile stair-case was backed up to the plane's forward hatch. The first man up the stairs opened the hatch and held it while the squad swept on to the plane, weapons raised. The scene on board was almost incomprehensible: there were uncon-scious bodies littering the aisles, and when they got to the President's office it only got stranger. The President was sitting in his chair, and open on the desk in front of him was the nuclear 'football'. On the floor was an uncon-scious young boy with snow-white hair who was wearing what looked like some sort of high-tech body armour. The President lifted his hands as far as he could, revealing that he was actually handcuffed to his chair.

'Would one of you gentlemen be kind enough to get me out of these things?' he asked.

☻ ☻ ☻

'Come in, I have something that I think you should see,' Nero said, gesturing for Raven to sit down on the other side of the desk. A large screen slid down from the ceiling on the other side of his office.

'This was recorded earlier, just before we arrived back at H.I.V.E.' Nero said.

'And now we go live to Kevin Harding, our Washington correspondent, who has the latest from Andrews Air Force Base,' the studio bound newscaster said, 'Kevin . . .'

'Thank you, Kim,' the reporter replied, behind him was a wire fence and a gated military checkpoint. 'There's still no official word from the White House as to what might have caused today's emergency landing of Air Force One, with a spokesman saying merely that contact with the plane had been lost due to "unforeseen technical difficulties." The spokesman went on to say that the President and all of the other passengers on board were fine but were receiving medical checks just to be on the safe side after problems developed with the ventilation system on board during the transatlantic flight.'

The report cut to footage of the President leaving the medical centre on the base and waving to crowds of journalists as he walked to his waiting car.

The reporter appeared on the screen again. 'While it is still not clear what the exact nature of the technical fault that caused the emergency landing was, one of the passengers, who wished to remain nameless, was quoted as saying that it was "quite a ride".'

'Thanks, Kevin,' the anchor replied with a smile. 'More on that story as we have it. In other news today, the controversial unscheduled nuclear test in Nevada yesterday continues to spur speculation –'

Nero pressed a button on the remote and the newscaster froze in mid-sentence.

'It didn't crash,' Raven said, sounding astonished.

'Apparently not, which, assuming he was still on board, would suggest that Otto may still be alive,' Nero said.

'If he's alive, I'm going to get him back,' Raven said without hesitation.

'Of course you are,' Nero replied, 'but first we have to find him. I have several of my sources within the US intelligence community working to establish Mr Malpense's current status and location. Unfortunately, the security surrounding any details of this event is rather tight at the moment, but I hope to find out more soon.'

'So they're going to cover it all up.'

'Yes, but that's hardly surprising. They are, understandably perhaps, keen to keep the news that their entire country was seconds away from armageddon as quiet as possible. It isn't the first time an event of this kind has been swept under the rug. As you well know, the vast majority of G.L.O.V.E.'s operations go unreported in the media. It isn't in the security forces' interests for people to know how often we are actually successful. G.L.O.V.E. may not have been responsible for this, not directly at least, but the principle is the same.'

'What about these Disciples that Drake mentioned?' Raven asked.

'It looks like we have some competition,' Nero said calmly. 'Rest assured that all of G.L.O.V.E.'s resources are being turned to finding out more about our new adversaries as quickly as possible. They will not catch us by surprise a second time. Jason Drake may now be beyond our reach but we are diverting all of our resources towards finding the rest of them. Pietor Furan especially – he has a great deal to answer for.'

'When the time comes, he's mine,' Raven said with something cold and deadly in her voice.

'That goes without saying,' Nero replied, 'given the history between the two of you.' A message window began to flash on the display on Nero's desk. 'I'm afraid you'll have to excuse me, Natalya, I have to take this call.'

Raven nodded and walked quickly out of his office. Nero tapped a key on his keyboard and Darkdoom's face appeared on the screen.

'Good afternoon, Max,' Darkdoom said, looking tired, 'I take it you've seen the news.'

'Yes, I was just discussing it with Raven,' Nero replied. 'There's a good chance that Mr Malpense is still alive after all.'

'Yes,' Darkdoom said, sounding slightly distracted, 'it

would appear so.'

'Is there something wrong?' Nero asked, picking up on his friend's mood.

'I've been thinking about the events Raven witnessed on the bridge of the Dreadnought.'

'Furan killing Drake?' Nero asked.

'No,' Darkdoom said, frowning. 'That just saved us the trouble of doing it. I'm more concerned by the fact that the Disciples had access to that organic computing technology – Animus, as he called it. Where did they get it from?'

'The only time we have seen anything similar was a few months ago when we tried to intercept H.O.P.E.'s transport train in the Alps. That substance was inert though. It may have been fully integrated within the structure of the train but it didn't appear to serve any purpose other than to foil Mr Malpense's abilities. The way it behaved on board the Dreadnought was different. What Raven described sounds like an evolution of that technology. Given the capabilities they have already demonstrated, I don't find it hard to believe that the Disciples might have stolen that technology and made their own modifications to it.'

'What if it wasn't stolen,' Darkdoom said. 'What if it was given to them?'

'H.O.P.E. and the Disciples working together?' Nero

asked, raising an eyebrow. 'Not a pleasant prospect.'

'No,' Darkdoom agreed, 'but certainly a possibility that warrants further investigation. I don't like being caught by surprise and that is exactly what the Disciples did. Whatever they have planned next I want to be one step ahead of them.'

'We should start by making sure they haven't turned anyone else on the ruling council,' Nero said. 'I'm reluctant to suggest that we start spying on our own people, but I don't see that we have much choice.'

'You're right,' Darkdoom replied with a nod, 'though I can't help but worry that this might be exactly what they want – suspicion and paranoia turning us against one another.'

'Trust is not something that comes easily in our business, Diabolus, you know that,' Nero said. 'We'll do whatever it takes to stop these people and that's all there is to it. If we've only learnt one thing from the past couple of days it's that the Disciples will stop at nothing to achieve their goals. If they're prepared to sacrifice a third of the planet's population to get what they want, then we have to be prepared to pay any price to stop them. G.L.O.V.E. has survived for all these years because we are subtle, discreet – the stiletto blade sliding between the plates of armour – and the Disciples, it would seem, are the exact opposite. They'll drag us all down with them if we let them. They have to be destroyed.'

'Agreed,' Darkdoom said. 'So what's our first move?'

☣ ☣ ☣

'You OK?' Shelby asked as she placed the tray with her lunch on it on the table and sat down next to Laura. The rest of the students in H.I.V.E.'s dining hall were chatting and laughing, oblivious to the events that had taken place less than twenty-four hours previously.

'What do you think?' Laura asked sadly, pushing the untouched food around her plate with a fork.

'Stupid question,' Shelby said, 'sorry.'

'If he'd just gone with Raven,' Laura said quietly, 'instead of being an idiot and trying to play the hero . . .'

'He probably saved hundreds of millions of lives,' Shelby said.

'What do I bloody care?' Laura snapped back at her.

'You don't mean that,' Shelby said, looking her in the eye.

'No . . . of course I don't, it's just . . .' Laura fought back the tears again. She'd had enough of crying. 'It's just so unfair,' she said sadly. 'After everything he did he should be a hero, but no one even knows and they're never going to.' Dr Nero had been quite clear about the fact that they were not to discuss any details of the recent situation with any of the rest of H.I.V.E.'s pupils. Otto's sacrifice was to remain a well-kept secret.

Lucy and Wing walked towards the table. Lucy was smiling broadly and even Wing looked like he was about to smile, something he certainly hadn't done since the Dreadnought.

'I don't think there's much to be happy about,' Shelby said angrily as they walked up to the table.

'Go on,' Lucy said excitedly, 'tell them what Raven just told us.'

'What's going on?' Laura asked quickly.

'Raven has just given me some interesting news,' Wing said, a definite smile appearing now. He sat down at the table and quietly recounted what Raven had just told him.

'He's alive!' Laura said with a gasp of astonished joy.

'They are not certain of that,' Wing said cautiously, 'but it looks like he may have survived, yes.'

'The only problem now is that nobody knows where he is,' Lucy said, 'not yet, at least.'

'So what do we do?' Shelby asked.

'I asked Raven the same thing and she told me that *we* do nothing and that we're to leave it to them to retrieve Otto,' Wing said, raising an eyebrow.

'And are we going to do that?' Laura asked.

'No, of course not,' Wing said with a tiny smile. 'Don't be ridiculous.'

Franz and Nigel came over and sat down at the table.

Franz appeared to have all three of that particular meal-time's options on his tray.

'What?' he asked as he saw Shelby staring at his tray. 'I have been in captivity. I am needing to be building up my strength again.'

'That's what you said at breakfast,' Nigel said with a sigh. He looked around the table. There were rather more smiles on people's faces than he had been expecting. 'Did we miss something?'

'Yes, as a matter of fact you did,' Wing replied cryptically. 'Let me ask you this: what do you think would be the best way to get off the island without anybody realising until it was too late?'

'Oh no,' Franz moaned, 'not again.'

A minute or two later as the hushed conversation at the table continued, a girl wearing the white overalls of a student from the Science and Technology stream came over to the table and pointed at the one empty seat.

'Is that seat taken?' she asked.

'Yeah,' Laura replied with a slight smile, 'I'm afraid it is.'

☹ ☹ ☹

The President looked through the window at the white-haired boy lying on the hospital bed in the other room. The boy had a drip going into one arm and a tube inserted into his nose but otherwise looked like he was just sound asleep.

'Talk to me,' the President said to the man standing next to him. 'Who is he?'

'His name is Otto Malpense,' the man replied, 'and he is affiliated with at least one terrorist organisation.'

'He's just a boy,' the President said with a frown.

'So are many suicide bombers, sir,' the man replied. 'The body armour he was wearing was highly sophisticated, real bleeding-edge stuff. The lab team at the Pentagon are going nuts over it.'

'Is he going to wake up?' the President asked.

'I don't know, sir. The doctors tell me they've never seen a coma quite like it. They say that his level of brain activity is astonishing. By all rights he should be awake and walking around, but, well, you can see for yourself that he isn't.'

'What happens if . . . when he wakes up?'

'We'll debrief him.

'No aggressive interrogations,' the President said firmly. 'Whoever he works for we owe that young man a great deal.'

'Understood, sir,' the man replied. 'Don't worry, he's in good hands.'

'Make sure that nothing happens to him,' the President instructed, staring at the man. 'I'll hold you personally responsible if it does. Do I make myself clear?'

'Perfectly, sir,' he replied.

The President took one last look at the boy on the bed and walked out of the room, secret-service agent in tow. The other man watched him leave and then walked through the door into the treatment room and over to Otto's bed. He pulled a syringe from his pocket and held it up, tapping the air bubbles out of the viscous black liquid inside and squeezing a tiny drop out of the needle. He jabbed the needle into the artery in Otto's neck and injected the contents of the syringe.

'It's so very good to see you again, Mr Malpense,' Sebastian Trent said with a vicious smile. 'We're going to do such great things together.'